ET

The Nimrod
Flip-Out

TRANSLATED FROM THE HEBREW BY
Miriam Shlesinger and
Sondra Silverston

VINTAGE BOOKS
London

Published by Vintage 2006

2 4 6 8 10 9 7 5 3 1

First published in Australia in 2004 by Picador

First published in Great Britain in 2005 by Chatto & Windus

Vintage
Random House, 20 Vauxhall Bridge Road, London SW1V 2SA

Random House Australia (Pty) Limited
20 Alfred Street, Milsons Point, Sydney, New South Wales 2061, Australia

Random House New Zealand Limited
18 Poland Road, Glenfield, Auckland 10, New Zealand

Random House (Pty) Limited
Isle of Houghton, Corner of Boundary Road & Carse O'Gowrie, Houghton, 2198, South Africa

The Random House Group Limited Reg. No. 954009
www.randomhouse.co.uk/vintage

A CIP catalogue record for this book is available from the British Library

ISBN 97800990497226 (from Jan 2007)
ISBN 0099497220

CONTENTS

FATSO

Surprised? Of course I was surprised. You go out with a girl. First date, second date, a restaurant here, a movie there, always just matinees. You start sleeping together, the fucks are dynamite, and pretty soon there's feeling too. And then, one day, she arrives all weepy, and you hug her and tell her to take it easy, that everything's okay. But she says she can't stand it anymore, she has this secret, not just a secret, something really awful, a curse, something she's been wanting to tell you the whole time, but she didn't have the guts. This thing, it's been weighing down on her like a ton of bricks, and now she's got to tell you, she's simply got to, but she knows that as soon as she does, you'll leave her, and

1

you'd be absolutely right too. And just after that, she starts crying all over again.

I won't leave you, you tell her. I won't. I love you. You may look a little upset, but you're not. And even if you are, it's about her crying, not about her secret. You know by now that these secrets that always make a woman fall to pieces are usually something along the lines of doing it with an animal, or with a Mormon, or with someone who paid her for it. I'm a whore, they always wind up saying. And you hug them and say, no you're not, you're not, or *shhh* . . . if they don't stop. It's something really terrible, she insists, as if she's picked up on how nonchalant you are about it, even though you've tried to hide it. In the pit of your stomach it may sound terrible, you tell her, but that's mostly because of the acoustics. Soon as you let it out it won't seem nearly as bad – you'll see. And she almost believes it. She hesitates a minute and then asks: what if I told you that at night I turn into a heavy, hairy man, with no neck, with a gold ring on his pinky? Would you still love me? And you tell her of course you would. What else can you say? That you wouldn't? She's simply trying to test you, to see whether you love her unconditionally – and you've always been a winner at tests. And sure enough, as soon as you say it, she melts, and you fuck, right there in the living-room. And afterwards, you lie there holding each other tight, and she cries, because she's so relieved, and you cry too. Go figure it out. And unlike all the other times, she doesn't get up and leave. She stays there and falls asleep. And you lie awake, looking at her beautiful body, at the sunset outside, at the moon appearing as if out of nowhere, at the silvery light flickering over her body, stroking the hair on her back. And within less than five minutes you find yourself lying next to this guy – this short fat guy. And the guy gets up and smiles at you, and dresses awkwardly. He leaves the room and you follow him, spellbound. He's in the den now, his thick fingers fiddling with the remote, zapping to the sports channels. Championship soccer. When they miss a pass, he curses the TV; when they score, he gets up and does this little victory dance.

After the game he tells you that his throat is dry and his stomach is growling. He could really use a beer and a nice hunk of meat. Well done if possible, and with lots of onion rings, but he'd settle for some pork chops too. So you get in the car and take him to this restaurant that he knows about. This new twist has you worried, it really does, but you have no idea what to do about it. Your command-and-control centers are down. You shift gears at the exit, in a daze. He's right there beside you in the passenger seat, tapping that gold-ringed pinky of his. At the next intersection, he rolls down his window, winks at you and yells at this chick who's trying to thumb a ride: Hey, baby, wanna play nanny goat and ride in the back? Later, the two of you pack in the steak and the chops and the onion rings till you're about to explode, and he enjoys every bite, and laughs like a baby. And all that time you keep telling yourself it's got to be a dream. A bizarre dream, yes, but definitely one that you'll snap out of any minute.

On the way back, you ask him where to let him off, and he pretends not to hear you, but he looks despondent. So you wind up taking him back home with you. It's almost 3 am. I'm gonna hit the sack, you tell him, and he waves to you, and stays in the beanbag, staring at the fashion channel. You wake up the next morning, exhausted, and with a slight stomach ache. And there she is, in the living room, still dozing. But by the time you've had your shower, she's up. She hugs you guiltily, and you're too embarrassed to say anything.

Time goes by and you're still together. The fucks just get better and better. She's not so young any-more, and neither are you, and suddenly you find yourselves talking about a baby. And at night, you and the fatso guy hit the town like you've never done before in your life. He takes you to restaurants and bars you didn't even know existed, and you dance on the tables together, and break plates like there's no tomorrow. He's really nice, the fatso guy, a little crass, especially with women, sometimes coming out with things that make you just wanna die. But other than that, he's great fun to be with. When you first met him, you didn't give a damn about soccer, but now you know every team. And whenever one of your favorites wins, you feel like you've made a wish and it's come true. Which is a pretty exceptional feeling for someone like you, who hardly knows what he wants most of the time. And so it goes: every night you fall asleep with him struggling to stay awake for the Argentinean finals, and in the morning there she is, the beautiful, forgiving woman that you also love till it hurts.

THE NIMROD FLIP-OUT

Miron freaks out

When it comes to Miron's problem, there are, as they say, several schools of thought. The doctors think it's some trauma he suffered when he was in the army that resurfaced all of a sudden in his brain, like a piece of shit you see floating in the toilet long after you've flushed. His parents are convinced it's all because of the mushrooms he ate in the East, which turned his brain to quiche. The guy who found him there and brought him back to Israel says it's because of this Dutch chick he met in Dharamsala, who broke his heart. And Miron himself says it's God who's messing everything up.

Latching onto his brain like a bat, telling it one thing, then the opposite, anything, just to pick a fight. According to Miron, after He created the world, God stayed awfully complacent for a couple of million years. Until Miron came along all of a sudden, and started asking questions, and God broke out in a sweat. Because God could tell straight off that, unlike the rest of humanity, Miron was no pushover. And as soon as you gave him the smallest opening, he'd slam right through it, and God – everyone knows – is really big on dishing it out, but not on taking it, and the last thing He can afford is a rebuttal, especially from a guy like Miron, and from the minute He realized it, He just kept driving Miron around the bend, hassling him whenever He could, with everything from bad dreams to girls who wouldn't put out. Anything, just so the guy would fall apart.

The doctors asked Uzi and me to help them a little with Miron's case history, because the three of us have known each other since day one. They asked us all kinds of questions about the army, about what had happened with Nimrod. But most of it we couldn't remember, and even the little bit that we did remember we didn't tell them because the truth was that they didn't look too nice, and Miron had told us a couple of things that bordered on *60 Minutes*. After that, during visiting hours, Miron begged us to bring him some hummus from the hunchback, because more than anything else, it was the food here that was doing him in. 'It's been three weeks since I got here,' he figured, 'and if you add that to the four months in the East, that's almost six months without hummus. I swear to you, I wouldn't wish that on my worst enemies.' So we went to get him some.

The hunchback said he didn't do takeaways. 'Only sit-downs,' he snarled in his half-menacing, half-indifferent tone. 'I'm not running a snack bar, y'know.' So we ordered a plate of hummus, and stuffed it in the pita ourselves. When we got back, Miron's mother was there. She said hi to Uzi, but not to me. She hasn't spoken to me for years, on account of me influencing her son to experiment with drugs. We didn't give him the hummus while she was still there, because we were afraid she'd tell the doctors or something. So we waited for her to leave. Meanwhile, the *ful* was getting cold, but that didn't matter to Miron, who wolfed it down. Three days later they discharged him. The doctors said his reaction to the medications was remarkable. Miron still insists it was on account of the hummus.

Uzi loses it

In June, Miron and me went down to Sinai. Uzi was supposed to come too, but he stood us up at the last second for some appointment with this German guy from a hi-tech company in Düsseldorf who could put up millions for a project in Uzi's company. It was supposed to be a kind of celebration, in honor of the fact that Miron wasn't considered crazy anymore, and Uzi felt a little uncomfortable with his childish attraction to money, so he promised that as soon as his appointment was over he'd join us there. 'I'll bet you anything he doesn't show,' Miron said. 'A double bet: first off, he won't show, and second, give him three more months and he'll marry the Turnip.' I didn't want to bet Miron about anything, because everything he said sounded depressing but pretty true. Turnip was our codename for Uzi's obnoxious girlfriend who was also deep into all those virtual hi-tech deals that Uzi loved to manage. I remember him asking us once why we called her Turnip, and Miron told him something about how it was because turnips are underrated: some people don't realize how good they are. Uzi didn't really buy it, but he never asked again after that.

If life is one big party, Sinai is definitely the chill-out. And even Miron and me, who hardly did anything in regular life anyway, could appreciate the ultimate veg-out nothingness of the place. Everywhere you looked on our beach there were these moonchild chicks, and Miron kept trying to come on to them and to make like he'd spent a lot of time in the East. It even worked now and then. Me, I didn't have the energy for that stuff, or the coordination either. So I just smoked bagfuls of grass, stared at the sea, and kept debating whether to order a pineapple pancake for lunch or to take my chances with the fish. I also kept an eye out for Miron from a distance, checking to see if he'd really straightened out. He still came up with some pretty weird stuff, like for instance when he insisted on taking a shit right near our hut because he was too lazy to walk all the way to the restaurant. But the truth is that he used to do stuff like that before he went crazy too.

'I have a hunch I'm going to get lucky with that short one with the navel stud,' he told me at night after we came back from the restaurant on the beach. 'You gotta admit, she's cute, isn't she?' The two of us were sitting around zonked, just staring out at the sea. 'Listen,' I told him, 'about that whole business when they put you away, I know that Uzi and me played it cool, but you scared the shit out of us.' Miron just shrugged. 'It was pretty freaky, like suddenly I started hearing voices – talking, singing. Like some broken radio that you can't figure out how to turn off. It drives you crazy. You can't think straight for a second. I'm telling you, I felt as if someone was trying to flip me out. And then it just stopped.' Miron took one more drag on his cigarette and put it out in the sand. 'And I'll tell you something else,' he said. 'I know this sounds a little whacked, but I think it was Nimrod.'

The next day, contrary to all our predictions, Uzi arrived. Too bad I didn't take Miron up on his bet. Soon as Uzi put his bag down in the hut he dragged us straight to the restaurant, chewed some squid and told us all about how the German guy had turned out to be even more of a pushover than he'd expected, and that he was happy to the max to be with us, with his best friends, in Sinai, his favorite place in the whole world. After that, he went charging up and down the beach, calling 'Yo Bro' at anything that moved, and hugging every Bedouin or Egyptian who wasn't fast enough to get away. When he got tired of that too, Uzi made us play backgammon with him, and after he beat both of us, he clobbered one of the Bedouins, and then he made the Bedouin traipse up and down the beach behind his bald opponent yelling, 'Watch out, girls, Abu-Gara's big.' Miron tried to cool him off with a puff, but that only made Uzi crazier. He began coming on strong to a forty-year-old American tourist, gave up in no time, ate three pancakes, told Miron and me that he couldn't get over the peace and quiet of the place, ordered kebab, and suggested that maybe the three of us and his new Bedouin friend, who turned out to be a taxi driver, could go down to play the casino at Tabba. Miron was dead-set against it, because he figured he was just about to make it with the babe with the navel stud, but Uzi was so worked up that Miron's horniness didn't stand a chance. 'No kidding,' Miron said soon as we got into the taxi, 'the guy's completely lost it.'

Abu-Gara and the Bedouin made a killing at Tabba, swooping down on one table after the next, leaving behind nothing but shattered croupiers and scorched earth. Between killings, Uzi wolfed down enormous slabs of apple pie and chocolate mousse cake. Miron and I just sat there, watching patiently, waiting for him to wear himself out. But to tell the truth, he just kept getting stronger and stronger. Once Uzi and the Bedouin had finished humiliating the casino and divvying up their winnings, we took the taxi to the border station. Miron and me reminded Uzi that we were supposed to be heading back, but he wouldn't hear of it. As far as he was concerned, the day was still young, and there was no reason not to cash in at a couple of clubs in Eilat before heading back. He made sure to give the Bedouin his business card, and they kissed about eighty times. Miron made one more try to persuade the Bedouin to take us back to the beach, leaving Uzi to continue his escapades on his own, but the Bedouin told us off and insisted that leaving a wonderful friend like Abu-Gara right in the middle of a celebration would be a disgrace, and he'd have loved to continue with us himself, except he wasn't allowed to cross the border. After that he kissed us too, got into the taxi and disappeared. When Uzi got tired of The Spiral, we went to the Yacht Pub and then to some hotel called the Blue Something, and only then, after Miron and me had refused twice to let him get some call girls sent up to our room, Uzi turned over on his stomach and started to snore.

Ever since that time in Sinai, Uzi's company's been on a roll. Apart from the German pushover, Uzi found two other suckers, one an American and the other from India, and it looked like he was about to knock the whole world on its ass. Miron said it only went to show how crazy all those business-people were. Because the fact was that ever since Uzi'd gone off the deep end he'd been getting bigger and bigger. Sometimes we'd still try to drag him with us to the beach or the pool hall, but even when he did come, he was so busy the whole time telling everyone how much he was enjoying it and what a great time we were having together, and checking the voicemail on his mobile that after an hour with him you'd simply lose the desire to live. 'Don't worry. He'll outgrow it,' I'd try to tell Miron, as Uzi got caught up in another transatlantic call just when it was his turn to shoot. 'Sure,' Miron would say in the tone of an ex-whacko who's got it all figured out, 'and if it's doing the rounds, you're next.'

Next in line to wig out

The next morning, I woke up in a complete panic. I had no idea what was causing it. I lay there, pressing my back to the mattress, trying not to move till I could figure out what had me so scared. But the more time went by, the less I knew about what had brought it on, and the more frightened I got. I lay there in bed frozen, and kept telling myself, in the second person, as calmly as I could, 'Take it easy, man, take it easy. This isn't really happening, it's just in your head.' But the thought that this thing, whatever it was, was inside my head made it a thousand times more horrifying. I decided to tell myself who I was, to say my name a few times in a row. That was bound to help me get a grip on myself. Except that even my name was gone all of a sudden. At least that got me up though. I crawled around the house, searching for bills, mail, anything with my name written on it. I opened the front door and looked at the other side of it where there's an orange sticker with the inscription: 'Have a hell of a life!' In the hallway there was the loud laughter of kids and the sound of footsteps approaching. I closed the door and leant against it.

15

Stay cool. In a minute I'd remember, or not. Maybe I never had a name. Whatever happens, that wasn't why I was sweating so much that my pulse was going to blow my brains out, that wasn't it, it was something else. 'Take it easy,' I whispered to myself again. 'Take it easy, whatever your name is. This can't go on much longer, it'll be over soon.'

Soon as it eased up a little, I phoned Uzi and Miron, and arranged to meet them both at the beach. It was only four hundred meters from my place, and I had no problem remembering how to get there, except that all the streets suddenly looked different, and I had to keep stopping to check the signs to make sure they were really the right ones. Not just the streets, everything looked different, even the sky was kind of squashed and low.

'I told you your turn would come,' Miron said and sucked at the red tip of his Wave-on-a-Stick popsicle. 'First I lost it, then Uzi.' 'I didn't lose it,' Uzi protested. 'I was just a little high, that's all.' 'Whatever you call it,' Miron went on. 'It's your turn now.' 'Ron isn't losing it either,' Uzi was beginning to get worked up. 'Why do you keep putting those ideas in his head?' 'Ron?' I asked. 'Is that my name?' 'Know what,' Uzi gave in, 'maybe he has lost it a little. Give us a bite.' Miron handed him the popsicle, knowing perfectly well he'd never see it again. 'Tell me,' he asked, 'when it started, didn't you feel there was someone in your head?' 'I don't know,' I hesitated. 'Maybe I did.' 'I'm telling you,' Miron whispered, as if it was a secret. 'I could feel him. He was saying things that only he could know. I'm sure it was Nimrod.'

Nimrod's flip-out

Until he turned twelve, Nimrod was a shitty person. The kind of whiner that, if he wasn't your best friend, you'd have socked him a long time ago. And then one day, just before his bar mitzvah, they put insoles in his shoes, and suddenly the guy was a whole new human being. The truth is that Miron, Uzi and me had been Nimrod's friends even before that, except that then, when he became nice too, it even began to be pleasant.

Later, in high school, Uzi and me were in the honors program, and Miron and Nimrod went to vocational school and mostly to the beach. Then came the army. Miron was drafted six months before us, and by the time our turn came he'd sucked up to enough people to make sure we would all be in the same unit with a cushy office job. Nimrod used to call it the padded pad.

Most of the time, we didn't do anything, except sit around in the canteen, threatening to file complaints against our commanders, and go home every day at five. Other than that, Uzi would surf at the Sheraton, I was forever jerking off, Miron took courses at the Open University, and Nimrod had a girlfriend. Nimrod's girlfriend was as good as they get, and because all of us except him were virgins, that made her even better. I remember I once asked Miron what he would do – hypothetically, I mean – if she came to his house, say, and asked him to fuck her. And Miron said he didn't know, but whatever he did, he'd regret it the rest of his life. Which is a nice answer but, knowing him, he'd be sure to take the fucking option first and the regretting option second.

But with Nimrod, it wasn't even that he was horny, he was simply in love with her. Her name was Netta, which is a name that I still love to this day, and she was a paramedic at the infirmary. Nimrod told me once that he could lie next to her in bed for hours without getting bored, and that the place he liked her to touch the most was the spot on his foot where everyone else's had an arch but his was flat.

At the base we would do guard duty twice a month, and once every two months we had to stay the weekend, which Nimrod always managed to arrange for days when Netta had infirmary duty so that even on guard duty they were together. A year and a half later, she left him. It was a strange kind of split, even she couldn't really explain why it happened, and after that Nimrod didn't care when his guard duty came out. One Saturday, Miron, Nimrod and I were on duty together. Uzi had just managed to forge some kind of a medical pass for himself. We were all on the same patrol – Miron first, Nimrod second, and me third. And even before I had a chance to replace him, this officer rushed in and said that the guy on duty had put a bullet in his head.

Round two

The second time Miron lost it, it was much more unpleasant. We didn't say a word about it to his parents, and I simply moved in with him till it passed. Most of the time, he was quiet, sitting in the corner and writing a kind of book to himself, which was supposed to eventually replace the Bible. Sometimes, when we'd run out of beer or cigarettes, he would swear at me a little, with conviction, and say that I was really a demon disguised as a friend, and that I'd been sent to torment him. But other than that, he was almost bearable.

Uzi, on the other hand, took his extended period of sanity very hard. He didn't admit it, but it seemed like he'd really had it with that sky-rocketing international company of his. Somehow, whenever he was in a flip, he had a lot more energy to write all kinds of dreary prospectuses and things and go to boring meetings. And now that he was a bit more sane, the whole businessman thing was a lot more of a drag. Even though it seemed as if his company was about to go public and he'd be raking in a couple of million with no extra effort.

Me, I'd been fired from another job, and Miron, in a lucid moment of being off beer and cheap fags, said that he was the one who'd gotten me fired with his unearthly spiritual powers. I don't know, maybe all those jobs just weren't for me, and I simply needed to sit it out till Uzi struck it rich and tossed me a little.

The second time Uzi started going bonkers proved once and for all that there was definitely a rotation thing going, and I started worrying because I knew I was next. Miron, who'd chilled out by then, kept insisting it had something to do with Nimrod. 'I don't know what he wants exactly. Maybe he wants us to even the score or something. But one thing's for sure, so long as we don't do it, whatever it is, I don't think it's going to stop.' 'Even what score?' I countered. 'Nimrod killed himself.' 'How do you know?' Miron wouldn't let it pass just like that. 'Maybe it was murder. Besides, maybe it isn't exactly vengeance. Maybe there's just something he wants us to do so he can rest in peace. You know, like in those horror films, where they open up a beer joint on an ancient burial ground, and as long as it stays there, the ghosts can't rest in peace.' In the end, we decided that Miron and I would go to the Kiryat Shaul Cemetery to make sure nobody had set up a Coke-and-mineral-water stand on Nimrod's grave by mistake. The only reason I agreed to go there with him was because I was really hyped about it being my turn soon. The truth was that, of the three of us, my crack-up was the worst.

Nimrod's grave had stayed exactly the same. We hadn't been there in six years. At first, on Memorial Day for the fallen soldiers, his mother still used to call us. But with all those military rabbis and those aunts who'd faint away every year, we weren't exactly keen on going. We kept telling ourselves that we would go some other day, on our own special memorial day, except that we always put it off. Last time we talked about it, Uzi said that actually every time we went to shoot pool together or took in a movie or a pub or whatever, it was a commemoration of Nimrod too, because when the three of us are together, then even if we're not exactly thinking about him, he's there.

It took Miron and me maybe an hour to find the grave, which actually seemed to be well tended and clean, with a couple of stones on top as proof that someone had been there not too long before. I looked at the dates on the grave and thought about how I was just about to turn thirty, and Nimrod wasn't even nineteen yet. It was kind of weird, because somehow, whenever I thought about him he was sort of my age, when in fact I hardly had any hair left and he was hardly more than a kid. On our way out, we returned the cardboard yarmulkes to the box by the gate, and Miron said he didn't have any more ideas, but that we could always have a séance. Outside the cemetery, on the other side of the fence, there was a fat, shaggy cat chewing a piece of meat. I looked at him and, as if he felt it, he looked up from the chunk of meat and smiled at me. It was a mean and ruthless smile, and he went back to chewing the meat without lowering his gaze. I felt the fear running through my body, from the hard part of my brain to the soft part of my bones. Miron didn't notice there was something wrong with me, and just continued talking. 'Relax, Ron,' I told myself. The fact that I remembered my name made me so happy that tears came to my eyes. 'Take a deep breath, don't fall apart. Whatever it is, it'll be over soon.' At that very moment, in the smelly office of some attorney in Petah Tikva, Uzi was chickening out of signing a deal that would transfer thirty-three per cent of his company's shares to an anonymous group of Polish investors for a million-and-a-half bucks. Think about it, if only he'd stayed flipped out for another fifteen minutes, he could have taken us and the Turnip on a Caribbean cruise, and instead he was making his way home on a number 54 bus from Petah Tikva with a creep of a driver who wouldn't even turn the air conditioning on.

Tri-li-li-li-la

When Uzi announced he was going to marry the Turnip, we hardly even put up an argument. Somehow we'd known it would happen. Uzi lied and said it was his idea, and that it was mainly so he could take out a mortgage from the bank for an apartment that he'd planned to buy anyway some place near Netanyah. 'How can you marry her?' Miron tried to reason with him, without much conviction. 'You don't even love her.' 'How can you say I don't love her?' Uzi protested. 'We've been together for three years. D'you know I've never cheated on her?' 'That's not because you love her,' Miron said, 'it's just because you're uncoordinated.' We were just shooting pool, and Uzi had clobbered both of us with the bullseye shots of someone who'd made up his mind to squeeze every drop out of the little bit of luck he still had left, quickly, before it had a chance to run out. There was only the eight-ball left, and it was Uzi's turn. 'Let's make a bet,' I offered Uzi in an act of desperation. 'If you pocket the eight-ball, Miron and I will never call her Turnip

23

again, ever. And if you miss, then you drop the whole wedding thing for a year.' 'When it comes to feelings, I never make bets,' Uzi said and pocketed the eight effortlessly. 'Besides,' he smiled, 'it's too late, we've already printed up the invitations.' 'How could you make him such a bet?' Miron told me off later. 'That shot was a sure thing.'

By the time the date rolled around, Uzi had managed to lose it two more times, and on both occasions he said he would call it all off, but changed his mind right away. As for me, I just crashed in Miron's apartment meanwhile. Now that we were wigged out most of the time, it was much nicer living together. And besides, I couldn't really afford my own place. Miron had stolen a big pile of wedding invitations from Uzi, and we would use them to make filters for joints. 'How can you go and marry someone whose mother's name is Yentl?' he would ask Uzi whenever we'd smoke a joint together, and Uzi would just stare at the ceiling and give that spaced-out laugh of his. The truth was that even though I was on Miron's side on this, I felt it wasn't much of an argument.

Three days before the wedding we held a séance. We bought a piece of blue construction paper, I drew all the letters on it with a black marker, and Miron got a glass from the kitchen, one of those cheap ones, and said he'd had it for ages, from his parents' house, and that Nimrod must have used it. We turned out all the lights and placed the glass in the middle of the board. Each of us put a finger on the glass, and we waited. After five minutes, Uzi got tired of it, and said he had to take a shit. He turned on the lights in the living room, found a week-old sports section, and locked himself in the bathroom. Miron and me rolled a joint. I asked Miron, if it had succeeded, and if the glass had moved, what did he expect to happen. That pissed Miron off, and he said it was too early to say it hadn't succeeded and that just because Uzi gets bored with everything so quickly, it doesn't mean that it won't work.

After Uzi finally came out of the bathroom, Miron switched off the lights again and asked all of us to concentrate. We put our fingers on the glass again, and waited. Nothing happened. Miron insisted that we try again, and nobody could work up the energy to argue with him. A few minutes later, the glass began to move. Slowly at first, but within seconds it was racing all over the board. Miron left his finger on it the whole time and kept writing down with his other hand each of the letters that it stopped on. T-r-i-l-i-l-i-l-i-l-a the glass hummed, and came to a smooth stop on the exclamation mark in the righthand corner of the page. We waited a while longer, and nothing happened. Uzi turned on the light. 'Tri-li-li-li-la, eh?' he said, annoyed. 'What are we, in kindergarten or something? You moved it, Miron, so don't you go pulling an Agent Mulder on me now. Tri-li-li-li-la? Godammit, okay. I'm dead beat. I've been up since seven. I'm going to sleep at Liraz's.' Liraz was the Turnip's name, and she lived close by. Even after Uzi had left, Miron kept staring at the page with the letters I'd drawn and I read a bit of the sports supplement that Uzi had taken to the bathroom, and when I had read it all, I told Miron I was going to get some shut-eye. Miron said okay, but that first he just wanted us to give one more chance to the thing with the glass, because no matter how much he thought about it, that Tri-li-li-li-la stuff didn't mean a thing to him. So we turned out the light again, and put the glass in place. This time it started moving straight away, and Miron wrote down the letters.

D-o-n-t-l-e-a-v-e-m-e-a-l-o-n-e the glass said, and then it stopped again.

Mazel tov

The wedding itself was awful, with a rabbi who thought he was a comedian and a DJ who played Enrique Iglesias and Ricky Martin. Miron actually met this girl there with a squeaky voice but a bod to kill for. After the ceremony, he even managed to get Uzi worried when he said that the glass he'd stepped on during the ceremony was the one they'd used for Nimrod's séance. While this was going on, I got another of my anxiety attacks and puked about two kilos of chopped liver into the toilet.

That same night, Uzi and the Turnip flew off on their honeymoon to the Seychelles Islands. Me and Miron sat on the balcony drinking coffee. Miron had a new thing going now. Whenever he'd make us coffee, he'd always make one instant for Nimrod too in the séance glass, and he'd put it on the table, the way you leave out a glass of wine for Elijah on Passover, and after we were through drinking, he'd spill it in the sink. Miron did a take-off of the DJ, and I laughed. The truth was that we were sad in a big way. You could call it chauvinist, possessive, ego-centric, lots of names, but the whole wedding thing weighed down on us like a ton of bricks.

I asked Miron to read me a chapter from that book of his, the one he writes whenever he flips, the one that's supposed to replace the Bible. The truth was that I'd asked him a million times, and he'd never do it. When he's flipped he's scared someone will steal his ideas, and when he's sane he's simply embarrassed. 'Come on,' I said, 'just read me a chapter, like a kind of bedtime story.' And Miron was so depressed that he agreed. He pulled a bunch of scribbled pages out of his shoe drawer. Before he started reading, he looked at me and said, 'You realize it's just the two of us left now, don't you? I mean, Uzi will still be one of us, and all, but he won't be part of Nimrod's rounds.' 'How can you tell?' I protested, though in my heart I'd thought of this even before he said it. 'Listen,' Miron said. 'Even Nimrod knows it isn't right to pick on someone who's married. The way he flips us out isn't always the best idea either, but the truth is that he wouldn't be doing it to us if he didn't feel in his heart that we agree. There's nothing we can do about it. We're screwed, Ron. There's just me and you, one week each, like kitchen duty.' Miron picked up the pile of pages and cleared his throat, like a radio announcer who chokes in the middle of reading the news. 'And if one of us suddenly goes?' I asked. 'Goes?' Miron looked up from his pages, confused. 'Goes where?' 'I don't know,' I smiled. 'Just goes. What if tomorrow the chick of my dreams comes on to me in the street, and we fall in love, and I marry her. Then you'd be the only one left to flip with Nimrod, full-time, alone.' 'Right.' Miron gulped down the last drops of his coffee. 'Good thing you're so ugly.'

SHOOTING TUVIA

To Shmulik

I got Tuvia for my ninth birthday from Raanan Zagoori, who was probably the cheapest kid in the whole class. He got lucky, and his dog had puppies right on the day of my party. There were four of them, and his uncle was going to dump them all in the river, so Raanan, who only cared about how not to spend anything on the class gift, took one of them and gave it to me. The puppy was tiny, with a bark that sounded more like a wheeze, but if anyone got on his case, he'd give a deep, low kind of growl that didn't sound anything like a puppy, and it was funny, like he was impersonating some other dog. Which is why I decided to name him Tuvia, after Tuvia Tsafir, this guy on TV who's always impersonating politicians.

From day one, my dad couldn't stand the sight of him. Tuvia didn't care much for Dad either. The truth is, Tuvia didn't like anyone much, except me. From the start, even when he was just a little runt, he'd bark at everyone. And when he grew a little bigger, he would snap at anyone who came too close. Even Mickey, who isn't the kind of guy who badmouths people, said my dog was messed up. Tuvia never snapped or did anything bad to me, though. He'd just keep jumping on me and licking me, and whenever I'd move away from him he'd start whining. Mickey said it didn't mean anything, because I was the one who fed him. But I've met lots of dogs who bark even at the people who feed them, and I knew that what Tuvia and I had going for us wasn't about food, and that he really did like me. He just did. For no reason. Go figure out a dog. But it was something strong. Fact is, my sister fed him too, but he hated her like hell.

In the morning, when I'd go to school, he'd want to come with me, but I'd make him stay behind because I was afraid he'd make a racket. We had a chain-link fence around our yard and sometimes, when I'd come home, I'd catch Tuvia still barking at some poor slob who dared to walk down our street.

He'd get so mad that he'd smash right into the fence. But the second he spotted me, he'd just melt. Right away, he'd start crawling on the ground, wagging his tail and barking about all the creeps who'd walked down our street and gotten on his nerves that day, and about how they were lucky they'd made it out of there. He'd already bitten a couple of them, but lucky for me they didn't complain, because even without that kind of thing, my dad was on Tuvia's case, just waiting for the chance to get rid of him.

Finally, it happened. Tuvia bit my sister, and they had to take her to the hospital for stitches. Soon as they got home, Dad took Tuvia to the car. I didn't need long to figure out what was going to happen, and I started crying, so Mom told Dad: 'C'mon Joshua, why don't you just forget it. It's the kid's dog. Just look at how upset he is.' Dad didn't say anything, just told my big brother to come with him. 'I need him too,' Mom tried. 'He's a watchdog, against thieves.' And my dad stopped short just before he got into the car, and said: 'What do you need a watchdog for? Did anyone ever try to steal anything in this neighborhood? What's to steal here anyway?' They dumped Tuvia in the river, and stuck around to watch him being washed away. I know, because my big brother told me so. I didn't talk to anyone about it, though, and except for the night they took him away, I didn't even cry at all.

Three days later, Tuvia turned up at school. I heard him barking from below. He was awfully dirty, and smelly too, but other than that he was just the same. I was proud of him for coming back. It proved that everything Mickey had said about his not really loving me wasn't true. Because if the thing between Tuvia and me had been just about food, he wouldn't have come right back to me. It was smart of him to come straight to school too. Because if he'd headed home without me, I don't know what my dad would've done. Even so, soon as we got to the house, Dad wanted to get rid of him. But Mom told him that maybe Tuvia had learned his lesson, and that maybe he'd behave himself now. So I hosed him down in the yard, and Dad said that from now on he'd be on a leash all the time, and that if he pulled anything again, that would be it.

Truth is, Tuvia didn't learn a thing from what happened. He just got a little crazier. And every day, when I'd come back from school, I'd see him barking like a maniac at anyone who happened to walk by. One day, I came home and he wasn't there, and Dad wasn't there either. Mom said they'd come from the Border Patrol because they'd heard he was such a feisty animal that they wanted to recruit him, and that now Tuvia was a scout-dog who'd track down terrorists trying to sneak across the border. I pretended to believe her. That evening, when Dad came back with the car, Mom whispered something in his ear, and he shook his head. He'd driven a hundred kilometers this time, all the way to Gedera, before setting Tuvia loose, just to make sure he wouldn't be able to come back. I know, because my big brother told me so. My brother also said it was because Tuvia had got loose that afternoon, and had managed to bite the dogcatcher.

A hundred kilometers is a long way, even by car, and on foot it's a thousand times more, especially for a dog, whose step is like a quarter of a human's. But three weeks later, Tuvia was back. He was there waiting for me at the school gate. Didn't even bark when he saw me, that's how exhausted he was, just wagged his tail without getting up. I brought him some water, and he must have lapped up about ten bowls. When Dad saw him, he couldn't believe it. 'A curse, that's what this dog is,' he told Mom, who quickly got Tuvia some bones from the kitchen. That evening I let him stay in my bed. He fell asleep before me, and all night long he just whined and growled, snapping at anyone who pissed him off in his dream.

In the end it was Grandma of all people that he had to pick on. He didn't even bite her. Just jumped on her, and knocked her over. She got a nasty bump on her head. Everyone helped her up. Me too. But then Mom sent me to the kitchen for a glass of water, and by the time I got back I saw Dad dragging Tuvia towards the car looking really mad. I didn't even try, and neither did Mom. We knew he had it coming. And Dad asked my brother to come along again, except that this time he told him to bring his M-16. My brother was just an army cook, but they issued him with a gun anyway. At first, he didn't catch on, and asked Dad what he needed a gun for. And Dad said it was to make Tuvia stop coming back.

They took him to the dump, and shot him in the head. My brother told me that Tuvia hadn't realized what was going to happen. He'd been in a good mood, and was turned on by all the neat stuff he found at the dump. And then, bang! From the second my brother told me, I hardly thought about Tuvia at all. All those other times, I couldn't get him out of my mind, and I'd keep trying to imagine where he was and what he was doing. But this time, there was nothing to imagine anymore, so I tried to think about him as little as possible.

Six months later he came back. He was waiting for me in the schoolyard. There was something wrong with one of his legs, his left eye was closed, and his jaw looked completely paralyzed. But as soon as he saw me, he seemed really happy, like nothing had ever happened. When I got him home, Dad wasn't back from work yet, and Mom wasn't there either, but even when they returned, they didn't say a thing. And that was it. Tuvia stayed from then on. Twelve more years. Eventually he died of old age. And he never bit anyone again. Every now and then, when someone would pass by our fence on a bike, or just make some noise, you could still see him getting worked up and trying to pounce, but somehow he always ran out of steam in the middle.

ONE KISS ON THE MOUTH

IN MOMBASA

For a minute, I got uptight. But she told me to take it easy, I had no reason. She'd marry me, and if it was important, because of our parents, it could even be in a hall. That wasn't the point. The point was somewhere else altogether – three years ago, in Mombasa, when she and Lihi went there after the army. Just the two of them went, because the guy who was her boyfriend had just re-enlisted. In Mombasa, they lived in the same place the whole time, some kind of guesthouse where a whole bunch of people hung out, mostly from Europe. Lihi wouldn't hear about leaving the place, because she'd just fallen in love with some German guy who lived in one of the cabins.

She didn't mind staying either, she was pretty much enjoying the quiet. And even though that guesthouse was exploding with drugs and hormones, no one hassled her – they could probably see that she wanted to be alone – no one except for some Dutch guy who got there maybe a day after they did and didn't leave the place until she went back home. And he didn't actually hassle her either, just looked at her a lot. That didn't bother her. He seemed like an all right guy, a little sad, but one of those sad types who don't complain. They were in Mombasa for three months, and she never heard him say a word. Except for once, a week before they left, and even then there was something so gentle about the way he talked to her, something so weightless, that it was as if he hadn't said anything at all.

She explained to him that the timing was bad, told him about her boyfriend, who was some technical something in the air force, about how they'd known each other since high school. And he just smiled and nodded and moved back to his regular spot on the steps of the hut. He didn't speak to her anymore, but kept on looking. Except that actually, now that she thought about it, he did speak to her one more time, on the day she flew back, and he said the funniest thing she'd ever heard. Something about how, between every two people in the world, there's a kiss. What he was actually trying to tell her was that he'd already been looking at her for three months and thinking about their kiss, how it would taste, how long it would last, how it would feel. And now she was leaving, and she had a boyfriend and everything, he understood, but just that kiss, he wanted to know if she would agree. It was awfully funny, the way he spoke, kind of confused, maybe because he didn't know English well, or he just wasn't much of a talker. But she said okay. And they kissed. And after that, he really didn't try anything and she came back to Israel with Lihi.

Her boyfriend was at the airport in his uniform to pick her up in his army car. They also moved in together, and to spice up their sex life a little they added some new things. They tied each other to the bed, dripped some wax, once they even tried to do it anally, which hurt like hell, and, in the middle, shit came out. In the end they split up, and when she started school she met me. And now, we're going to get married. She has no problem with that.

She said I should pick the hall and the date and whatever I want, because it really doesn't matter to her. That isn't the point at all. Neither is that Dutch guy, I have nothing to be jealous of there. He's probably dead already from an overdose or else he's lying drunk on some sidewalk in Amsterdam, or he went and got a Master's degree in something, which sounds even worse. In any case, it's not about him at all, it's that time in Mombasa. For three months, a person sits and looks at you, imagining a kiss.

YOUR MAN

When Abigail told me she wanted us to break up, I was in shock. The cab had just pulled up at her place, and she got out on the sidewalk side, and said she didn't want me to come up, and that she didn't really want to talk about it either, and that most of all she never wanted to hear from me again, not even a Happy New Year or a birthday card. And then she slammed the cab door so hard that the driver cursed her through the window. I just sat there in the back seat, numb. If we'd had a fight or something, maybe I'd have been more prepared for it, but it had been a really great evening. The movie wasn't that hot, but other than that everything was cool. And then that monologue, out of nowhere, and the door slamming, and bam! Our whole six months together gone, just like that! 'So what now?' the driver asked, looking at me in the rear view mirror. 'Want me to take you home? If you've got a home, that is. To your parents' place? Friends? A massage parlor downtown? You're the boss, you're the king.' I didn't know what I was going to do with myself. All I knew was that it wasn't fair. After Ronit and I split up I swore I wouldn't let anyone get close enough to hurt me like that, but then Abigail came onto the scene, and everything was so good, and I just didn't deserve this. 'You're right,' the driver grunted. He'd turned off the ignition and tilted his seat back. 'Why drive when it's so cozy here. Me, I don't care. The meter's running either way.' And that's when they announced the address on the radio. 'Nine Massada Street. Who's up?' And that address – I'd heard it before, and it stayed in my memory as if someone had scratched it in there with a nail.

When Ronit split it was the same, in a cab, the cab that was taking her to the airport, to be precise. She said it was over between us and, sure enough, I never heard from her again. I was left that way then too, stuck alone in the back seat of a cab. The driver that time yakked and yakked, and I didn't hear a word. But that annoying address on the radio I actually do remember very clearly. 'Nine Massada

Street. Whose call?' And now, maybe it's just a coincidence, but still, I told the driver to go there, I had to find out what that address was all about. As we pulled up, I saw another cab drive away, and, inside, in the back seat, was the silhouette of a small head, like a child's or a baby's. I paid the driver and got out.

It was a private home. I opened the gate, and walked down the path leading to the door. I rang the bell. It was a pretty dopey thing to do, and I don't know what I'd have done if anyone had opened the door, or what I would have said. There was no reason for me to be there at that hour. But I was so mad I didn't care. I rang once again, a long ring, and then I banged on the door, like in the army when we used to do door-to-door searches, but nobody came. In my head, thoughts about Abigail and Ronit began to get all mixed up with thoughts about other breakups, and everything sort of got lumped together. And this house, where nobody opened the door, was getting on my nerves. I started to circle it, looking for a window I could peep through. The place didn't have any windows, just a back door, mostly glass. I tried to look inside – everything was dark. I kept trying, but I couldn't get my eyes to adjust. It seemed as if the harder I tried, the blacker it all looked. It blew my mind, it really did. And suddenly I saw myself as if I was out of my body – bending over, lifting a rock, wrapping it in my sweatshirt and breaking the glass.

I reached in, careful not to cut myself, and opened the door. I groped for the light switch, and when I found it, the light was yellow and dim. One bulb for that whole big room. And that's exactly what the place was – an enormous room, no furniture, completely empty, except for one wall that was covered with photographs of women. Some of them were framed, some just stuck on the wall with masking tape, and I knew them all: there was Dalia, my girlfriend in the army; and Danielle, we went steady in high school; and Stephanie, a tourist who stayed; and Ronit. They were all there, and in the lefthand corner, in a delicate gold frame, was a picture of Abigail, smiling. I turned out the light and collapsed in the corner, trembling all over. I didn't know the guy who was living here, why he was doing this to me, or how he always succeeded in wrecking things. But suddenly it all fell into place, all those breakups, jumping ship out of the blue – Danielle, Abigail, Ronit. It was never about us, it was always him.

I don't know how much time went by before he arrived. First I heard the cab pulling away, then the sound of his key in the front door, and then the light went back on, and there he was, standing right in front of me and smiling, the son of a bitch, just looking at me and smiling. He was short, like a kid, with big eyes, no lashes, and he was holding a colored plastic schoolbag. When I got up out of my corner he just gave a weird little laugh, like he'd been caught red-handed, and asked how I'd gotten there. 'So she left too, eh?' he said when I'd come closer. 'Never mind, there'll always be another one.' And me, instead of answering, I slammed the rock down on his head, and when he dropped I didn't stop. I don't want another one, I want Abigail, I want him to stop laughing. And the whole time I was bashing him with the rock, he just kept whimpering: 'What're you doing, what're you doing, what're you doing, I'm your man, your man,' till he stopped. When it was over, I threw up. And when I'd finished throwing up, I felt lighter, sort of, like on army hikes when it's someone else's turn to take the stretcher from you, and suddenly you feel light – lighter than you ever thought possible. Light as a child. And all the hatred and the guilt and the fear that I'd be caught – it all just disappeared.

Behind the house, not far away, were some woods, and that's where I dumped him. The rock and the sweatshirt, which were all full of blood, I buried in the yard. In the weeks after that, I kept looking for him in the papers, both in the news and in the missing persons ads; but there was nothing. Abigail didn't answer my messages, and someone at

45

work told me they'd seen her in town with this tall guy with a ponytail. It broke me up to hear that, but I knew there was nothing I could do about it, it was over for good. A little while later, I started going out with Mia. Right from the start, everything with her was so sane, so okay. And unlike the way I usually am with girls, with her I was very open right from the start, no defenses. Sometimes at night I'd dream about that dwarf, how I got rid of his body in the woods, and I'd wake up in a panic, but then I'd remind myself there was no reason, he wasn't around anymore, and then I'd hold Mia and go back to sleep.

Mia and I broke up in a cab. She said that I had no feelings, that I was clueless, that sometimes she could be suffering like crazy, and I'd be sure she was having a good time, just because I was. She said we'd been having problems for quite a while, but that I hadn't even noticed. And then she started to cry. I tried to take her in my arms, but she pulled away and said that if I cared about her I should just let her go. I didn't know if I should go up after her, and keep trying. On the cab radio they gave an address: 'Four Adler Road.' I told the driver to take me there. Another cab was already standing there when we arrived. A couple got in, about my age, maybe a little younger. Their driver said something, and they both laughed. I kept going, to nine

Massada Street. I looked for his body in the woods, but it wasn't there. The only thing I could find was a rusty iron rod. I picked it up and started walking towards the house.

The house looked just the same, dark, with the broken pane in the back door. I reached inside, groped for the handle, taking care not to get cut. I found the light switch right away. It was still all empty, except for the pictures on the wall, the dwarf's ugly schoolbag and a dark, sticky stain on the floor. I studied the pictures. They were all there, in exactly the same order. When I was through with the pictures, I opened the bag and looked inside. There was some cash, a used bus pass, an eyeglass case, and a picture of Mia. In it, her hair was up, and she looked a little lonely. And suddenly I understood what he'd said back then, before he died, about there always being another one. I tried to picture him on the night Abigail and I broke up, going wherever it was he went, returning with the picture, making sure, I don't know how, that I'd meet Mia. Except I'd managed to blow it again this time. And now it wasn't so sure I'd ever meet another one. Because my man was dead. I'd killed him myself.

ONE GOOD DEED A DAY

For Uzi and Omer

There was that old black guy in San Diego who bled all over the upholstery when we took him to the hospital, and that fat homeless lady in Oregon that Avihai left his ugly sweatshirt for, the one with the Signal Corps insignia he got when he finished the radio operators' course, and there was a kid in Vegas who cried so hard his eyes were falling out. He said he'd lost everything and he needed a bus ticket and, at first, Avihai didn't want to give him anything because he said it was a con, and there was the cat with the eye infection in Atlanta that we stopped to buy milk for. There were a lot, I don't even remember them all, most of them were no big deal, small stuff, like stopping for a hitchhiker or leaving a big tip for an old waitress. One good deed a day. Avihai said it was good for our karma, and anyone doing the States coast-to-coast like we were needed good karma. Not that the States is some kind of dangerous jungle in South America, or a leper colony in the middle of India, but still.

We got to Philadelphia a second before the end of the trip. From Philadelphia we planned to go on to New Jersey. Avihai had a friend there who'd promised to help us sell the car. From there, I was scheduled to go to New York and back home. Avihai planned to stay another few months in New York and find a job. It had been a fantastic trip. Better than we planned. With skiing in Reno and alligators in Florida and you name it, all for four thousand dollars a person. And honestly, even though we cut corners sometimes, we went all out for the really important things. In Philadelphia, Avihai dragged me to a boring natural history museum that his friend from New Jersey said was cool. From there, we went to have lunch at a Chinese place that had a great-smelling buffet, all you can eat for $6.99.

'Hey, don't leave your car here,' some skinny black guy who looked completely strung out yelled at us. He got up off the sidewalk and walked towards us. 'Park cross the street, or they gonna strip it in a second. You lucky I caught you in time.' I said thanks and started walking towards the car, but Avihai told me to wait a second, that the black guy was bull-shitting us. The black guy got really uptight when I stopped, and also because of the weird language we were speaking, and said again to move the car or else they'd trash it, and that it was good advice, ter-rific advice, advice that'd save us our whole car, and advice like that was worth at least five dollars. Five dollars for someone who'd keep our car in one piece for us. Five dollars for a hungry war veteran and God would bless us. I wanted to get out of there, that story of his with the car really wiped me out, because it made me look pretty dumb, but Avihai kept talking to him. 'You're hungry?' Avihai asked him. 'So come and eat with us.' We had this rule that we didn't give money to junkies so they couldn't spend it on another fix. Avihai put a hand on his shoulder and tried to lead him to the restaurant. 'I don't like Chinese,' the black guy pulled back, 'come on guys, gimme a fiver. Don't be mean, today's my birthday. I saved your car for you. I wanna I wanna I wanna eat good on my birthday.' 'Congratulations,' Avihai smiled, patient as always, 'a birthday should be celebrated. Come on, tell us what you feel like and we'll go eat with you.' 'I feel like feel like feel like feel like,' the black guy swayed, 'come on, gimme me a fiver. Please, don't be like that, it's really far.' 'No problem,' I told him, 'we have a car, we'll drive there together.' 'You don't believe me, huh?' the black guy continued, 'You think I'm a liar. That ain't nice. Not after I done saved your car for you. That ain't no way to treat someone on his birthday. You're mean mean mean. You ain't got no heart.' And all of a sudden, from out of the blue, he started crying. The both of us stood there, next to the skinny black guy who was crying. Avihai shook his head at me, but even so, I pulled a ten dollar bill out of my pouch. 'Here, take it,' I told him, and then I added, 'We're sorry,' even though I didn't exactly know for what. But the black guy wouldn't touch the money, just cried and cried, and said we'd called him a liar and we had no heart and that's no way to treat a war veteran. I tried to shove the bill into one of his pockets, but he wouldn't let me get close and just kept walking back-wards. At some point, he started to really take off in a kind of slow, swaying run, cursing and crying harder with every step.

After we ate at the Chinese buffet, we went to see the Liberty Bell, which is supposed to be one of America's most important historical sites. We waited in line for three hours and, in the end, when we got there, they showed us this ugly bell that someone famous rang when the Americans declared their independence, or something like that. At night, in the motel, Avihai and I counted the money we had left. With the three thousand dollars we thought we could get for the car, we had almost five thousand. I told him I didn't care if he kept it all and gave me my share when we got back home. Avihai said that first we should sell the car and then we'd see. He stayed in the room to watch a sci-fi series, and I went over to the AM–PM store across from the motel to get us some coffee. When I came out of the store, I saw a huge full moon above me. But really huge. I'd never seen such a moon before. 'Big, huh?' said a skinny guy with red eyes and pimples who was sitting on the steps of the store. He was wearing a short T-shirt with a picture of Madonna on it, and his arms were lined with needle tracks. 'Huge,' I said, 'I never saw a moon like that.' 'Biggest in the world,' the skinny guy said and tried to get up. 'You wanna buy it? For you, twenty bucks.' 'Ten,' I said, and handed him the bill. 'You know what?' The skinny guy's smile showed a mouth of rotten teeth. 'Make it ten, you look like a nice guy.'

SHRIKI

Meet Reuven Shriki. An out-of-sight guy. Really awesome. Someone who had the guts to live the dreams most of us don't even dare to dream. Shriki's rolling in money, but that's not the point. He also has a girlfriend, a French model, who posed in the nude for the world's best slick magazine – if you didn't jerk off with it, that was just because you couldn't get your hands on it – but that's not what makes him the man either. What's special about Shriki is that, unlike others who made it big, he's not smarter than you, not better looking than you, not better connected or shrewder than you, he isn't even luckier than you. Shriki is exactly, I mean exactly, like me and you – in every way. And that's

55

what makes you so jealous – how did someone who's like us get so far? And anyone who tries to say it was the timing or the odds is full of crap. Shriki's secret is much simpler: he made it because he took his ordinariness as far as it could go. Instead of denying it or being ashamed of it, Shriki said to himself, this is who I am, and that's all there is to it. He didn't try to make himself more or less than he was, he just flowed with it, *naturel*. He invented ordinary things, and I stress, ordinary. Not brilliant, just ordinary, and that's exactly what humanity needs. Brilliant inventions might be good for brilliant people, but how many brilliant people are there? On the other hand, ordinary inventions arc good for everyone.

One day, Shriki was sitting in his living room eating olives filled with pimentos. He didn't find the filled olives very fulfilling. He liked the olives themselves much more than the pimento filling but, on the other hand, he preferred the pimento to the original hard, bitter pit. And that's how it came to him – the first in a series of ideas that would change his life and ours – olive-filled olives, that's all, an olive without a pit, filled with another olive. It took the idea a little while to catch on, but when it did, it refused to let go, like a pit bull clamping its jaws on its victim's ankle. And right after the olive-filled olives came avocado-filled avocados and, finally, the sweet crowning glory, apricot-filled apricots. In less than six years, the word 'pit' lost one of its meanings. And Shriki, of course, became a millionaire. After he cleaned up in the food business, Shriki moved on to real estate, and with no special vision there either. He just made sure to buy where it was expensive, and, guess what, within a year or two, it got even more expensive. That's how Shriki's assets grew, and with time he found himself investing in almost everything, except hi-tech, a field that put him off for reasons so primal he couldn't even express them in words.

As it does with every ordinary person, money changed Shriki. He got more cheeky, more cheery, more feely, more beefy, in short, more everything. People didn't adore him, but they didn't abhor him either, which is nothing to sneeze at. Once, during a TV interview that was a bit too personal, the interviewer asked Shriki whether he thought a lot of people aspired to be like him. 'They don't have to aspire,' Shriki smiled, half at the interviewer, half to himself, 'they already are like me,' and the studio filled with the sound of wild applause booming from the special electronic device the show's producers had purchased especially for up-front answers just like that one.

Imagine Shriki sitting in an armchair on the deck of his private pool, trailing a piece of pita through a plate of hummus, drinking a glass of freshly squeezed fruit juice, as his curvy girlfriend sunbathes naked on an air mattress. And now try to imagine yourselves in his place, sipping the freshly squeezed juice, tossing some sweet nothing to the naked French girl. A snap, right? And now try to imagine Shriki in your place, exactly where you are, reading this story, thinking about you there in his mansion, imagining himself sitting beside the pool in your place, and zap! Here you are again reading a story, and he's back there. Ordinary as hell, or as his French girlfriend likes to say, *naturel-naturel*, eating another olive and not even spitting out the pit, because there is none.

EIGHT PER CENT OF
NOTHING

Benny Brokerage had been waiting for them in the doorway for almost half an hour, and when they arrived he tried to act as if it didn't make him mad. 'It's all her fault,' the older man sniggered and held out his hand for a firm, no-nonsense shake. 'Don't believe Butchie,' the peroxide urged him. She looked at least fifteen years younger than her man. 'We got here earlier, except we couldn't find any parking.' And Benny Brokerage gave her his foxy smile, like he really gave a shit why she and Butchie were late. He showed them the furnished apartment, with its high ceiling and a kitchen window that almost gave you a view of the sea. He'd barely gotten through half the usual round when Butchie pulled out his checkbook and said he'd take it, and that he was even okay with paying a year's rent up front, except that he wanted a bit off the top, just to feel he wasn't being taken for a ride. Benny Brokerage explained that the owner was living abroad, so he wasn't at liberty to lower the price. Butchie insisted it was small change. 'As far as I'm concerned,' he said, 'you can take it off your commission. What's your cut?' 'Eight,' Benny Brokerage said after a moment's pause, preferring not to risk a lie. 'So you'll still be left with five,' Butchie announced, and finished writing out the check. When he saw that the broker wasn't holding out his hand to take it, he added, 'Look at it this way, the market's in the cellar, and five per cent of something is a lot more than eight per cent of nothing.'

Butchie, or Tuvia Minster, which was the name that appeared on the check, said the peroxide would drop by the next morning to pick up an extra key. Benny Brokerage said no problem, except it had to be before eleven, because he had some appointments after that. The next day, she didn't show. It was 11.20 already, and Benny Brokerage, who was aching to leave but didn't really want to stand her up, pulled the check out of the drawer. It had the office phone numbers, but he preferred to avoid another tedious conversation with Butchie, and went for the home number instead. It wasn't until she answered that he remembered he didn't even know her name, so he opted for 'Mrs. Minster'. She somehow sounded a little less dumb on the phone, but she still couldn't remember who he was or that they'd made an appointment for that morning. Benny Brokerage kept his cool, and reminded her slowly, the way you do when you're talking to a child, how he had met with her and her husband the day before, and how they'd signed for the apartment. There was no response at the other end and when she finally asked him to describe what she looked like, he realized he'd really blown it. 'The truth is,' he crooned, 'that I must have the wrong number. What did you say your husband's name is? That's it then. I was looking for Nissim and Dalia. Those 411 people messed me up again. I'm really sorry. Goodbye,' and he slammed the receiver down before she had a chance to answer. The peroxide arrived at the office fifteen minutes later, eyes at half-mast and a face that hadn't been washed yet. 'I'm sorry,' she yawned. 'It took me half an hour to find a cab.'

The following morning, when he arrived at the office, there was a woman waiting outside on the side-walk. She looked about forty, and something about the way she was dressed, about her fragrance, was so not-from-around-here that when he spoke he instinctively went for his most genteel pronunciation. Turned out she was looking for a two- or three-room place. She'd prefer to buy, but she didn't rule out a rental, as long as it was available right away. Benny Brokerage said he did happen to have a few nice apartments for sale, and that because the market was in a slump they would be reasonably priced too. He asked her how she'd found him, and she said she'd looked in the Yellow Pages. 'Are you Benny?' she asked. He said no – that there hadn't been a Benny for ages, but that he'd kept the name in order not to lose the goodwill. 'I'm Michael,' he smiled. 'The truth is that when I'm on the job, even I forget sometimes.' 'I'm Leah,' the woman smiled back. 'Leah Minster. We spoke on the phone yesterday.'

'This is a little uncomfortable,' Leah Minster said all of a sudden, out of nowhere. The first apartment had been too dark, and they were walking through the second one. Benny Brokerage tried to play dumb, and started talking about how simple it would be to renovate, and stuff like that, as if she'd been referring to the apartment. 'After you phoned me,' Leah Minster ignored his reply, 'I tried to talk it over with him. At first he lied, but then he got tired of it, and confessed. That's what the apartment is for. I'm leaving him.' Benny Brokerage continued showing her around, thinking to himself that it was none of his business, and that there was no reason for him to get uptight. 'Is she young?' Leah Minster persisted, and he nodded and said:

'She's not nearly as pretty as you. I hate having to say a thing like this about a client, but he's an idiot.'

The third apartment had better light, and when he showed her the view of the park from the bedroom window, he felt her moving closer, not touching him exactly, but close enough. And even though she liked the apartment, she wanted him to show her another one. In the car, she kept asking him all sorts of questions about the peroxide, and Benny Brokerage tried to put her down but to stay kind of vague at the same time. He didn't really feel comfortable with it, but he went on, because he saw it was making her happy. Whenever they stopped talking, there was a kind of tension, especially at the stop lights, and somehow he just couldn't think of anything to say, the way he usually could, a little story that would take their minds off being stuck. All he could do was stare at the traffic light and wait for it to change. At one of the intersections, even when the light changed, the car in front of them, a Mercedes, didn't move. Benny Brokerage slammed the horn twice and cursed the driver through the window. And when the guy in the Mercedes didn't seem to give a damn, he stormed out of the car. Turned out there was nobody to pick a fight with, though, because the driver, who seemed at first to be dozing, didn't wake up, even when Benny Brokerage nudged him. Then the ambulance crew arrived and said it was a stroke. They searched the driver's pockets and the car, but they couldn't find any ID. And Benny Brokerage felt kind of rotten for cursing the guy without a name, and he was sorry for the mean things he'd said about the peroxide, too, even though that really had nothing to do with it.

Leah Minster sat beside him in the car, looking pale. He drove her back to the office and made them both some coffee. 'The truth is that I didn't tell him anything,' she said, and took a sip of the instant. 'I was lying actually, just so you'd tell me about her. I'm sorry, but I just had to find out.' Benny Brokerage smiled, and told himself and her that there was no harm done really, that all they'd done was see a couple of apartments and some poor guy who'd dropped dead, and that if there was anything to be learned from the whole experience it was that thank God they were alive, or something along those lines. She finished her coffee, said sorry again, and left. And Michael, who still had a few sips to go, looked around his office, a two-by-three cubicle with a window, overlooking the main drag. Suddenly the place seemed so small and transparent, like the ant colony he got for his bar mitzvah a million years ago. And all the goodwill that he'd boasted about so solemnly just two hours earlier also sounded like crap. Lately, it had begun bothering him that people called him Benny.

PRIDE AND JOY

By the end of the first term, Ehud Guznik was already the tallest boy in his class, maybe even in the whole grade. And besides that, he had a new sports bike, a squat, hairy dog with the eyes of one of those old men who's been waiting on line at the public health clinic all morning, a girlfriend from his class who wouldn't kiss on the mouth but let him touch the boobs she didn't have, and a straight-A report card, except for geography, and even that was because the teacher was a bitch. In short, Ehud had nothing to complain about, and his parents were bursting with pride. You couldn't bump into them without having to listen to a little anecdote about their amazing child. And people, like people, would nod at them in a mixture of boredom and genuine admiration, and say, 'Wonderful, Mr./Mrs. Guznik, that's really wonderful.'

But what really counts isn't what people say to your face. It's what they say behind your back. And behind their backs, the first thing people said about Max and Felicia Guznik was that they kept getting smaller. Over a single winter, they seemed to have lost at least fifteen centimeters per head. Mrs. Guznik, once considered imposing, now barely reached the breakfast cereal shelf in the grocery store, and Max, too, who once stood close to a meter-eighty, had already moved the car seat all the way forward so he could reach the gas pedal. Very unpleasant, and the whole business just became more obvious next to their giant of a son, only a fourth-grader, but already a head taller than his mommy.

Every Tuesday afternoon, Ehud went to the schoolyard with his father to play basketball. Ehud's father thought Ehud had great potential, because he was both tall and smart. 'All through history, the Jews were always considered a smart people, but very short,' he liked to explain to Ehud while they practiced shooting baskets, 'and even once in a blue moon, when a big schlub did get born, for some reason, he always turned out to be such a knucklehead that you couldn't even teach him what a hook shot is.' But you could teach Ehud, and he got better from week to week. And lately, ever since his father started getting shorter, they were evenly matched. 'You,' his father would tell him on the way home from the court, 'you will be a great player some day, the Moshe Dayan of basketball, except without the patch.'

The compliments made Ehud very proud, even though he'd never seen that Moshe Dayan play, but even more than he was proud, he was worried. Worried about the scary way his parents were getting shorter. 'Maybe all parents are like that,' he sometimes tried to reassure himself out loud, 'and next year, they'll teach us about it in science class.' But deep in his heart, he knew something was wrong. Especially after Netta, who'd said yes when he asked her to go steady with him five months before, swore to him on the Bible that her parents, from the time she was little, had stayed more or less the same height. The truth was that he wanted to talk to them about it, but he felt there were things it was better not to talk about. Netta, for example, had a kind of light fuzz on her cheeks, like a beard, and Ehud always pretended he didn't notice, because he thought maybe she herself didn't know, and if he told her, she'd just feel bad. Maybe it was the same thing with his parents. Or even if they did know, maybe they were still glad he didn't notice. Things went on like that until after Passover. Ehud's parents kept getting smaller, and he kept acting as if nothing was happening. And the truth is that no one would ever have figured it out if it hadn't been for Zayde.

From the time he was a puppy, Ehud's dog was attracted to old people. And that's why his favorite thing was walking in King David Park, where all the old people from the retirement home went to get some air. Zayde could sit next to them and listen to their long stories for hours. They were also the ones who gave him the name 'Zayde', a name he liked a whole lot better than the original 'Jimmy' he got at the pound. Of all the old men, Zayde's favorite was an old geezer in a billed cap who talked to him in Yiddish and fed him blood sausage. Ehud also liked that old man, who made Ehud swear, the first time they met, never to get on an elevator with Zayde because, according to him, dogs don't understand the concept of an elevator, and going into a kind of small room in one place, and then seeing the doors open on another place altogether, shakes their confidence in their spatial perception and, in general, makes them feel really inferior. He didn't offer Ehud any blood sausage, but he did treat him to jelly beans and chocolate coins wrapped in gold. That old man must have died, or moved to a different home, because they didn't see him in the park anymore. Sometimes Zayde still barked and ran after a different old man who looked enough like him, and then he whimpered a little when he found out he was wrong, but that was all.

One day, after Passover, Ehud came home from school in a lousy mood, and when he finished walking Zayde, he didn't feel like going up the stairs, so they got on the elevator. He felt a little guilty as he pressed the 4 button, but said to himself that the old man was probably dead anyway, which definitely meant he didn't have to keep his promise. When the elevator door opened, Zayde peered out, walked back into the elevator, contemplated for a second, and fainted dead away.

Ehud and his frightened parents went straight to the vet, who quickly reassured them about the dog. But that vet was much more than your ordinary vet. He was a family doctor and a gynaecologist from South America who, at some point in his life, for personal reasons, had decided to treat animals. And that doctor needed only one look to realize that the Guzniks were suffering from a rare family disease, a disease that resulted in Ehud's growing taller and taller, but at his parents' expense. 'It's simple math,' the vet explained. 'Every centimeter added on to the child is a centimeter subtracted from the parents.' 'And this disease,' Ehud probed, 'when does it end?' 'End?' The vet tried to camouflage his sorrow with a thick Argentinean accent. 'Only when the parents disappear.'

All the way home, Ehud cried and his parents tried to comfort him. Strangely enough, their terrible fate didn't bother them at all. In fact, they even seemed to enjoy it a little. 'Lots of parents are dying to sacrifice everything for their children,' his mother explained to him when he was already in bed, 'but not all of them get the chance. Do you know how awful it is to be like Aunt Bella, who sees her son growing up to be short, stupid and untalented, just like his father, and she can't do a thing about it? Okay, it's true that, in the end, we'll be gone, but so what? In the end, everyone dies, and your father and me, we won't even die, we'll just disappear.'

The next day, Ehud went to school without really feeling like it, and got thrown out of Bible class again. He was sitting on the steps near the gym feeling sorry for himself when he suddenly realized something: if every centimeter he grew was at his parents' expense, all he had to do to save them was to stop growing! Ehud hurried to the nurse's office and slyly asked for all the information she had on the subject. From all the brochures she shoved at him, Ehud learned that if he wanted to put up a real fight against growing, what he had to do was smoke a lot, eat little and not regularly, and sleep even less, preferably with lots of interruptions.

He gave his ten-o'clock-recess sandwich to Shiri,

a nice, chubby girl from the other fourth-grade class. He ate as little as he could at meals, and to keep people from suspecting, he always passed the meat and dessert to his faithful dog, who waited under the table with sad eyes. The sleeping thing worked out by itself, because since that meeting with the vet, he couldn't sleep more than ten minutes anyway without some scary, guilt-filled dream waking him up. Which left the business with the cigarettes. He smoked two packs a day of cheap, unfiltered cigarettes. Two whole packs, not one cigarette less. His eyes got red and his mouth filled with a bitter taste, and he also started to cough, an old-man's cough, but not for a minute did he think of stopping.

A year and something later, on the day report cards were formally handed out, Matt Zlotnitski and Raz Samara were already taller than he was. Raz also became Netta's new boyfriend after she dumped Ehud because of the bad breath he'd developed. In fact, Ehud got a little unpopular that year. To tell the truth, the kids stopped talking to him completely because they said his chronic cough got on their nerves and, besides, his marks were going down and he wasn't good at sports anymore. The only one who still spoke to him was Shiri, who had started out liking him because of the sandwiches, but later took to him because of his personality and other things, and they spent hours together, talking about all kinds of stuff he'd never talked about with Netta. Ehud's parents stopped shrinking at fifteen centimeters, and after the doctor confirmed it, Ehud even tried to stop smoking, but couldn't. He went to an acupuncturist and a hypnotist, and they both said that the main reason he couldn't stop was pampering and character, but Shiri, who actually liked the smell of the cigarettes, consoled him by saying that it really didn't matter.

On Saturdays, Ehud would put his parents in his shirt pocket and take them for a bike ride. He pedaled slowly enough for the stout Zayde to keep up with them, and when his parents fought inside his pocket, or just got tired of each other, he would move one of them to another pocket. Once, Shiri even went with them, and they rode to the park and had a real picnic. And on the way back, when they stopped to look at the sunset, Ehud's father whispered loudly to him from his pocket, 'Kiss her, kiss her,' which was a little embarrassing. Ehud quickly changed the subject and talked to her about the sun and how hot and big it was and all kinds of things like that, until it was dark, and his parents fell asleep deep in his pocket. When he'd exhausted all his stories about the sun and they'd almost reached Shiri's house, he told her about the moon and the stars too, and their effect on each other, and when those stories were finished too, he coughed and shut up. And Shiri said to him, 'Kiss me,' and he kissed her. 'Way to go, son!' he could hear his father whisper from the depths of his pocket and feel his emotional mother jab him with her elbow and cry softly with joy.

SURPRISE EGG

To Danny, with love

This is a true story. Three months ago a woman, about thirty-two years old, met her death in a suicide bomb attack near a bus stop. She wasn't the only one who met her death, lots of others did too. But this story is about her.

People who are killed in terrorist attacks are taken to the Forensic Institute in Abu-Kabir for an autopsy. Many key figures in Israeli society have wondered about this procedure, and even the people who work at Abu-Kabir don't always understand it exactly. Everyone knows the cause of death in those attacks, and a body isn't some surprise egg that you open without knowing what you're going to find inside – a sailboat maybe, or a race car or a plastic koala. Whenever they operate they always find the same things, after all – little pieces of metal, nails, or other kinds of shrapnel. Very few surprises. But in the case of the thirty-two-year-old woman, they did find something else. Inside her body, besides all those pieces of metal that had torn into her flesh, this woman had dozens of tumors, really big ones. There were tumors in her stomach, in her liver and in her intestines, but especially in her head. When the pathologist peeked into her skull, the first thing he said was 'Oh my God' because it was simply frightening. He saw dozens of tumors that had inched their way into her brain like a swarm of cruel ants that just wanted to devour more and more.

And this is where the scientific observation comes in: if this woman hadn't died in a terrorist attack, she would have collapsed within a week and would have died from her tumors within a month, two months tops. It's hard to see how a young woman like that could have been suffering from such an advanced cancer without its being diagnosed at all. Maybe she was one of those people who don't like medical examinations or maybe she figured the pain and the dizziness she'd been having were something routine that would just go away. In any case, when her husband arrived to identify her at the morgue, the pathologist had a hard time deciding whether to tell him about it or not. On the one hand, it was a revelation that could have offered some comfort – there's no point in tormenting yourself with thoughts like 'If only she hadn't gone to work that day' or 'If only I'd driven her' when you know that your wife was about to die anyway. On the other hand, this news could make the grief even more distressing and turn her arbitrary and horrible death into something much more horrible: a death experienced twice over in a sense, making it inevitable, as if someone up there wanted to make absolutely sure, and no what-ifs could have saved her, not even hypothetically. Then again, the pathologist thought to himself, what difference does it really make? The woman's dead, her husband's a widower, her children are orphans, that's what matters, that's what's sad, and all the rest is nonsense.

The husband asked to identify his wife by her foot. Most people identify their loved ones by their faces. But he asked to identify her by her foot, because he thought that if he saw her dead face, the sight would haunt him his whole life, or rather, what remained of it. He had loved her and he knew her so well that he could identify her by each and every part of her body, and somehow her foot seemed the most remote, neutral and far removed. He looked at the foot for another few seconds, even after he'd identified the barely visible wavy contours of her toe-nails, the slightly crooked, chubby big toe, the perfect arching of her sole. Maybe it was a bad idea, he thought to himself as he continued to look at the little foot (size 6), maybe it was a bad idea to choose the foot. A dead person's face looks like a sleeping person's, but with a dead person's foot there's no mistaking the death lurking under every toenail. 'That's her,' he told the pathologist after a while, and left the room.

Among the people at the woman's funeral was the pathologist. He wasn't the only one; the Mayor of Jerusalem was there, and the Minister of Internal Security. Both of them made personal promises to the husband, repeating his first name and the deceased woman's name many times as they spoke, to avenge her cruel death. They gave a dramatic and vivid description of how they would hunt down those responsible for dispatching the murderer (there was, after all, no way of taking revenge on the suicide bomber himself). The husband looked rather uneasy with all those promises. It seemed that he wasn't all that interested, and the only reason he was trying to hide it was to avoid hurting the feelings of all those impassioned public figures who were naive enough to believe that their vehement speeches could offer him some solace.

The funeral was the second time the pathologist

had considered the idea of telling the husband that his wife had been on the verge of death in any case, to offset some of the uneasiness and vengefulness in the air, but this time too he kept it to himself. On his way back, he tried to think philosophically about everything that had happened. What is cancer, he thought to himself, if not a terrorist attack from above? What is it that God is doing, if not terrorizing us in protest against . . . something. Something so lofty and transcendental that it is beyond our grasp? Like most of his work at the institute, this thought too was surgically precise, but it didn't really make any difference.

The night after the funeral, the husband had a sad dream in which the dead foot was rubbing against his face, a dream which caused him to wake up in a state of fright and agitation. He tiptoed into the kitchen, so as not to wake the children, and made himself a cup of tea without turning on the light. Even after he'd finished drinking the steaming tea, he went on sitting in the dark kitchen. He tried to think of something he would like to do, something that would make him happy, anything. Even things he couldn't really allow himself because of the kids or because he couldn't afford to, but nothing came to mind. He felt full of a dense and sour substance that was blocking his chest, and it wasn't grief. It was something much more serious than grief. After all those years, life now seemed like no more than a trap, a maze, not even a maze, just a room that was all walls, no door. There must be something, he persisted, something I'd like to happen even if I can't possibly make it, anything.

Some people commit suicide after someone close to them goes, others turn to religion, and there are those who sit in the kitchen all night and don't even wait for the sun to rise. The light from outside was beginning to creep into the apartment and pretty soon the little ones would be waking up. He tried to recall once more the feel of the foot in his dream, and the way it always happens with dreams, all he could do was reconstruct it but not really experience it. 'If only she hadn't gone to work that day,' he thought, forcing himself to get up, 'if only I'd driven her. She'd still be alive now, sitting here in the kitchen with me.'

DIRT

So let's say I'm dead now, or I open a self-service laundrette, the first one in Israel. I rent a small place, a little run-down, on the south side, and paint everything blue. At first, there are only four machines and a special dispenser that sells tokens. Then I put in a TV and even a pinball machine. Or else I'm on my bathroom floor with a bullet in my head. My father finds me. At first, he doesn't notice the blood. He thinks I'm dozing or playing one of my stupid games with him. It's only when he touches the back of my neck and feels something hot and sticky oozing from his fingers towards his arm that he realizes something's wrong. People who come to do their wash in a self-service laundrette are lonely people. You don't have to be a genius to figure that out. And me, I'm really no genius, and I did. That's why I always try to create an atmosphere in the laundrette that will make people feel less lonely. Lots of TVs. Dispensers that say thank you in a human voice for buying the tokens, pictures of mass rallies on the walls. The tables for folding laundry are set up so that lots of people have to use them at the same time. Not because I'm stingy, it's on purpose. Lots of couples met at my place because of those tables. People who used to be lonely and now they have someone, maybe more than one, who lies next to them at night, shoves them in their sleep. The first thing my father does is wash his hands. Only then does he call for an ambulance. That hand washing is going to cost him dearly. He won't forgive himself till his dying day. He'll even be ashamed to tell people. How his son is lying there next to him, dying, and he, instead of feeling grief or compassion or fear, something, all he can feel is revulsion. That laundrette will turn into a chain. A chain that'll be big, especially in Tel Aviv, but it'll do well in the suburbs too. The logic behind its success will be simple – wherever there are lonely people and dirty laundry, they'll always come to me. After my mother dies, even my father will come into one of those branches to do his laundry. He'll never meet a woman or make a friend there, but the chance that he might will push him to go there every single time, will give him a tiny sliver of hope.

DORABLE

The first thing that made him suspicious was the smell. It wasn't that she suddenly had an other-man smell, like a heavy aftershave or hairy sweat. It was just that she'd always had such a subtle smell, the kind you barely noticed, and suddenly it had become so strong it made his head spin. Besides, she kept disappearing – not for long. Fifteen minutes maybe, or a little longer, and then she'd be back, like nothing had happened. The time it really got to him was when once, right in the middle of the evening news, she came in and asked him if he had change for a hundred. He took out his wallet, slowly, suspiciously, and pulled out two fifties. 'Thanks,' she said, and gave him a peck on the cheek. 'You're welcome,' he said, 'but hey, why do you need change all of a sudden, in the middle of the night?' 'No reason really,' she smiled. 'Just felt like it.' And she disappeared towards the kitchen porch.

It's not that they fucked less often. People say that's a sure giveaway. And when they did, it was as passionate as ever. She didn't ask him for more money either, which is another tip-off. The opposite, in fact: she became more economical. And their talks – well, the truth is they'd never talked much anyway – so there wasn't anything about that to make him suspicious either. And yet, he could tell there was something going on. A dark secret – so dark that there was black under her fingernails, like in those movies where in the end you discover that your wife is a hooker, or a Mossad agent, or something like that.

He could have followed her, but he preferred to wait and see. Maybe he was afraid of what he'd find out. Until one day, when he came home from work with a migraine in the middle of the day and parked his car at the entrance to their driveway, a silver Mitsubishi with a big pro-life bumper sticker pulled up behind him and started honking away. 'Hey you,' the Mitsubishi shouted. 'Get that car out of there. Can't you see you're blocking the way?' The truth was that there wasn't much to block in the entrance to his own driveway, but without giving it much thought, he moved a little to the side and let the Mitsubishi get by. As he got out of the car he thought that maybe, despite his splitting headache, he ought to try and find out what the pro-lifer was doing in his yard. But before he could get very far, he spotted her, right there in the middle of their neglected backyard, just where he'd once promised her he'd plant a mulberry tree. She was wearing dirty blue overalls, and leaning over the Mitsubishi with a fuel hose in her hand. He looked up and saw that the hose led right into a fuel pump. Next to the fuel pump was an air pump, and between the two was a little booth with a sign in childish lettering that said: 'FUEL – CHEAP!' 'Fill 'er up! Fill 'er up!' he heard the driver shout. 'Fill 'er up till she chokes!' He stared at her for a minute or so. She didn't see him, because she had her back turned, and when the fuel pump rang because the tank was full, he stiffened, like someone waking up out of a bad dream, got into his car, and drove back to work, as if nothing had happened.

He didn't discuss it with her, even though he often had the urge. He just kept quiet, and waited for her to bring it up. Suddenly, everything made sense: the smell, the dirt, those short disappearances of hers. There was just one thing he couldn't figure out. Why hadn't she shared it with him? And no matter how hard he tried to explain it to himself, he could feel the pain welling up inside. There's something insulting about a loved one who opens up a business behind your back, no matter what the explanation or the psychology. You can't help it. It just hurts, and that's that. Next time she asked him if he could break a hundred, he said he couldn't, even though his wallet was bulging with twenties and fifties. 'Sorry,' he pretended to sympathize. 'What did you say you needed it for?' 'No reason really,' she smiled. 'I dunno, I just had this urge.' And then she just disappeared onto the porch. Bitch.

She didn't run the business on her own. She had a helper, an Arab. He knew because he followed her a little. Once, when she was out shopping, he even drove up, like an ordinary customer, and talked with Sami – that's what he wanted people to call him – which was almost short for Samir. 'It's nice, this filling station of yours,' he sucked up to Sami. 'Gee, thanks,' Sami said, 'but it's not all mine. She and I each have half.' 'You married?' he pretended. 'You bet,' Sami nodded, and started pulling some snaps of his kids out of his wallet, but then he realized, and stopped, and explained that his partner wasn't his wife. She was someone else. 'Too bad my partner isn't here,' Sami smiled. 'You'd love her. She's dorable.'

He'd been to the station lots of times since then, always when she was away. He even got kind of friendly with Sami. Sami had a degree in philosophy and psychology, and it's not that he understood things about the world any better because of what he'd studied, but at least he could name all the things he didn't understand. 'Say,' he asked Sami once, 'if you were to find out that somebody close to you was hiding something from you, not cheating on you, but still hiding something, what would you do?' 'I don't think I'd do anything,' Sami said. 'Gee,' he said, 'why's that?' 'Because I wouldn't know what to do anyway,' Sami answered without thinking, the way people do with really easy questions.

The years went by, and they had a kid. Two kids even, identical twins. Towards the end of her pregnancy the station was really humming, and he'd help Sami out, without her knowing. The twins were dorable too, and bursting with energy. When they got a little older, they started fighting a lot, but you could always tell how much they really loved each other. When they were about nine, one of them lost an eye in a fight with the other one, and they stopped being identical. And their parents, who were really proud of them, would play with them whenever they could. Sometimes he was sorry he hadn't planted that mulberry tree when he promised he would. Kids love climbing, after all, and berries. But he never mentioned it. In fact, he wasn't angry at her anymore, and always gave her change when he had it, no questions asked.

GLITTERY EYES

This is a story about a little girl who loved glittery things more than anything else in the whole world. She had a dress with glitters, and socks with glitters, and ballet slippers with glitters. And a black doll called Christie, named after their maid, with glitters. Even her teeth glittered, though her father insisted that they sparkled, which wasn't quite the same thing. 'Glittery,' she thought to herself, 'is the color of fairy godmothers, and that's why it's the prettiest color of all.'

On 'Make-Believe Day' in kindergarten, she dressed up as a fairy godmother, and sprinkled glitters over everyone who came near her, and said it was wishing powder. If you mixed it with water, it would make your wish come true, and if they went home right away and mixed with water, then their wishes would come true too. It was a very real-looking costume, and it won her first prize in the costume competition. And the teacher, Lily, said that if she hadn't known her from before, if she just saw her by chance on the street, she would be sure the little girl was a real fairy godmother.

When the little girl got home, she took off her costume, stood there in nothing but her undies, threw all of her glitters in the air, and shouted: 'I want glittery eyes!' She shouted it so loud that her mother came running to see if everything was all right. 'I want glittery eyes,' the little girl said, quietly this time, and kept on saying it the whole time she was in the shower, but even after that, when her mother dried her off and helped her into her pajamas, her eyes stayed ordinary. Very very green, and very very pretty, but not glittery. 'With glittery eyes, I'd be able to do so many things,' she tried to persuade her mother, who seemed to be losing her patience. 'I'd be able to walk along the street at night, and the drivers would see me from far away, and when I got older, I'd be able to read in the dark and save a lot on electricity, and when-ever you lost me at the movies you'd always be able to find me right away, without calling the usher.' 'What's all this nonsense about glittery eyes?' her mother said, and pulled out a cigarette. 'There's no such thing anyway. Who put that ridiculous idea in your head?' 'Yes, there is!' the little girl shouted, and jumped up and down on her bed. 'There is, there is, there is, and besides, you're not supposed to smoke next to me, because it's not good for me.' 'Okay,' her mother said, 'okay. Look, it isn't even lit.' And she put the cigarette back. 'Now, get into bed like a good girl, and tell me who's been talking to you about glittery eyes. Don't tell me it's that fat teacher of yours?' 'She isn't fat,' the little girl said, 'and it wasn't her. Nobody talked to me about it. I saw it for myself. There's this dirty little boy in our kindergarten class and he has them.' 'And what's the dirty little boy's name?' 'I don't know,' the little girl shrugged. 'He's kind of dirty and he always sits quietly far away from everyone. But his eyes glitter, that's for sure. And I want eyes like that too.' 'So go over to him tomorrow and ask him where he got them,' her mother suggested, 'and when he tells you, we'll go there, and get them for you too.' 'And until tomorrow?' the little girl asked. 'Until tomorrow, go to sleep,' her mother said, 'and I'll go outside for a smoke.'

The next day, the little girl made her father take her to kindergarten really really early, because she just couldn't wait any longer, and she wanted to ask the dirty little boy where she could get glittery eyes.

But it didn't do her any good, because the dirty little boy arrived last, long after everyone else. And today he wasn't even dirty. His clothes were still a little old, and they had spots on them, but he himself looked like he'd washed, and even his hair was almost combed. 'Tell me,' she turned to him without a second's hesitation, 'where do you get such glittery eyes?' 'It's not on purpose,' the almost-combed little boy apologized. 'It just happens.' 'And what do I have to do for it to just happen to me too?' the little girl cried out. 'I think you need to want something an awful lot, and when it still doesn't happen, your eyes become glittery, just like that.' 'That's stupid,' the girl said, getting angry. 'Look, I want glittery eyes an awful lot, and it doesn't happen, so why aren't my eyes glittery?' 'I don't know,' the boy said, frightened because she was angry, 'I only know about myself, not about others.' 'I'm sorry I yelled,' she reassured him, touching him with her tiny hand. 'Maybe you only have to want certain kinds of things. Tell me, what did you want so badly, and you didn't get?' 'A girl,' the boy stammered. 'To be my girlfriend.' 'Is that all?' the little girl exclaimed. 'But that's easy. Tell me who she is and I'll make her become your girlfriend. And if she won't, I'll make sure nobody talks to her anymore.' 'I can't,' the little boy said. 'I'm too shy.' 'All right,' the little girl said. 'It doesn't really matter.

And it wouldn't solve my problem anyway, or get me glittery eyes. Besides, that could never happen to me. If I ever wanted someone to be my girlfriend, they'd want to, because they all want to be my girl-friend.' 'You,' the little boy blurted out, 'I want you to be my girlfriend.'

For a few seconds, the little girl didn't say any-thing, because the dirty little boy had managed to surprise her. Then she touched him again with her tiny hand and explained, in a voice that her father used whenever she tried to run across the street or to touch something electrical, 'But I can't be your girlfriend, because I'm very smart and popular, and you're just a dirty little boy who always sits quietly far away from everyone and the only thing that's special about you is that you have glittery eyes, and even that will disappear now if I agree to be your girlfriend. Though I have to admit that today you're a lot less dirty than usual.' 'I mixed with water,' the less-dirty little boy admitted, 'to make my wish come true.' 'Sorry,' the little girl said, running out of patience, and went back to her seat.

All that day, the little girl felt sad, because she understood that she would probably never have glittery eyes. And none of the stories or the songs or the show-and-tell could make her feel any better. And every now and then, when she almost suc-ceeded in not thinking about it, she'd see the little boy standing at the far end of the kindergarten, looking at her quietly, and his eyes just became more and more glittery, as if out of spite.

TEDDY TRUNK

I'm driving south on the old road, towards Ashdod. In the passenger seat next to me is Teddy Trunk, listening to a tape and drumming on the dashboard. He knows this road like the palm of his hand, from the time before the army, when he lived around here and used to drive to Tel Aviv with his friends every Saturday night. They're the ones who gave him that name, 'Teddy Trunk'. Today, no one calls him that anymore, not even just 'Teddy'. Today, most people call him 'Mr Schuler' or 'Schuler'. His wife calls him 'Theodore'. I don't think he really likes her to call him that.

We're on our way to a local council near Gedera to close a deal. I should probably say that he's closing a deal and I'm driving him there. That's my job. I'm a driver. I once had a route delivering dairy products, which is much more money, but I just wasn't into getting up at four every morning and arguing with all those cheapskate grocers about small change. Teddy once told me I'm a person without ambition, and that he's jealous of me because of it. I think that was the only time I felt like he was patronizing me. Most of the time, he's actually okay.

On my very first day on the job, I opened the car door for him and he told me not to open doors for him, and also that he always sits in the front, even when he's reading or looking over papers. When we'd stop to eat, he always paid. I wasn't really crazy about that, and in the end we agreed that for every five times he paid, I'd pay once, because he earns about five times more than I do. That was his idea, and I said fine, because it sounded logical.

The first time I treated was at a steak place in some gas station in the south. Shitty food, and the waiter, right before we paid, pegged him. 'Well what do you know, I should drop dead if it isn't Teddy Trunk.' Teddy kind of smiled at the waiter and nodded, but I saw he wasn't too thrilled about seeing him. We had an arrangement that if one of us paid, the other left the tip, and on the way out, I noticed that he didn't leave the waiter anything.

'What a creep,' I said to him later in the car. 'Why?

He happens to be a pretty nice guy,' he said, without really meaning it, 'maybe the best student in our grade. Funny he's stuck here as a waiter.' I wanted to ask him about the tip, but it seemed a little out of line, so I asked about the name instead. 'I don't like that name,' he said instead of answering, 'don't ever call me that, okay?'

That evening, before I dropped him off, he softened up a little and told me that when he was a kid, he was once late for school. In the hallway, someone said he should tell the teacher his father drove him there and on the way, something in the car broke down. And that's what he did. And when the teacher asked him what exactly broke down in the car, little Teddy told her that the trunk had broken down – and he was thrown out of class.

Ever since that story, even though I keep calling him 'Schuler', I can't think about him with any other name but 'Teddy Trunk'. 'I'm going to charge him such a price, that Shimshon, that it'll make his yarmulke spin,' Teddy says and drums on the dashboard in time to the song on the radio. 'Those guys on the local council here pretend to be hard up, but they're loaded.' After his meeting, we decided to have supper in a Russian restaurant around here that people said is something else. Teddy Trunk's treat. I might even have a few drinks, not too many, because I still have to drive to Tel Aviv later.

When he goes into his meeting, I park the car. The steering wheel hadn't felt right to me the whole way, and now I see that one of the front tires is almost flat. A spare I had, but the jack was gone. I might've made it to Tel Aviv that way, but I had time to kill anyway. 'Hey kid,' I say to a skinny boy bouncing a ball in the yard, 'go ask your father if he has a jack.' The kid runs home and comes back with someone wearing shorts and flip-flops. 'Tell me something, asshole,' flip-flops says, waving his car keys at me, 'why the hell should I help you with a jack?' 'Because it's happier and more fun when people are nice to each other,' I try a little milk-of-human-kindness on him. And they say small town people are nicer. 'You don't remember me, huh?' he says, taking his jack out of his car and tossing it to the ground near my feet. 'Two pork chops, one Coke, one Diet Coke, one Bavarian Cream with two spoons. Never heard of a tip, did you, Mr Nice Guy?' And then it hits me, the guy who waited on Teddy Trunk and me. He's actually nice, curses a little, but helps me with the tire. I'm a screw-up at that stuff. 'One helluva car,' he tells me when we're finished, and when I tell him that I'm only the driver, he looks surprised. 'So in the restaurant, you were with your boss,' he smiles, 'Teddy Trunk – your boss? Good for him, poor guy.'

His kid comes back with a family-sized bottle of

Coke with almost no fizz, and two glasses. 'Did he ever tell you why they call him Teddy Trunk?' Flip-Flops asks, pouring me a glass. I nod. 'What assholes we were, eh?' he laughs a pretty ugly laugh. 'Do you still sometimes drive with him in the trunk, just for old-times' sake?' Then, when he sees I don't understand, he tells me about how in high school, they were a gang of six, and every Saturday night they'd go to Tel Aviv together. Five in the car, and Teddy. 'He used to curl up in the trunk, like this, in his going-out clothes,' Flip-Flops smiles, 'and we'd close the trunk and didn't open it till we got to Tel Aviv. And later, on the way back, the same thing. Did you ever ride in a trunk, all boozed up?' I shake my head. 'Me neither,' he takes the empty glass from me. 'Well, at least now he rides in the front.'

I'm driving north on the old road, towards Tel Aviv. In the passenger seat next to me is Teddy Trunk, listening to a tape and drumming on the dashboard. He knows this road like the palm of his hand, from the time before the army when he lived around here and used to drive to Tel Aviv with his friends every Saturday night. They're the ones who gave him that name, 'Teddy Trunk'. Today, no one calls him that anymore.

MALFFUNCTION

I think my computer is ffucked up. I don't think it's the computer itselff actually, just the keyboard. I bought it not long ago, reffurbished, ffrom the classiffieds. The guy who sold it to me was weird. Opened the door wearing a silk robe and a ffedora, like some classy hooker in a black-and-white art ffilm. Made me some tea with mint that he grew in the window box. 'The computer's a steal,' he said. 'You won't regret it.' So I gave him ffive hundred, and now I do. The ad said they were selling everything because they were going on a long trip, but the guy in the ffedora gave me the real reason: he was going to drop dead any minute ffrom some disease, except that that's not something you write in an ad, especially not iff you want people to come. 'The truth is,' he said, 'that death is a bit like a trip to somewhere, so it isn't ffalse advertising.' As he said it, he had a quivery voice, optimistic like, as though ffor a second he'd managed to picture death as a happy-go-lucky class trip to a new place, and not just some good-ffor-nothing darkness that's breathing down your neck. 'Does it come with a warranty?' I asked, and he laughed. I meant it seriously, but when he laughed, I ffelt awkward, so I pretended like it was meant to be ffunny.

MAN WITHOUT A HEAD

In the bushes behind our school's basket-ball court, they found a man without a head. I say 'they', like it was a million people, but it was only my cousin, Gilad, whose ball flew into the bushes by mistake. And he told me that it was the most disgusting thing he'd ever seen. Because the ball landed exactly where the head was supposed to be, and when he bent down to pick it up, a kind of wet lizard came out of the hole of the dead guy's neck and scooted up his arm. That was so disgusting that afterwards he had to wash his hands in the fountain for half an hour and, even then, his hands still had this smell of rotten food.

The police said on TV that it was murder. The

truth? You don't have to be Colombo to figure that out. A person doesn't end up without a head from a sickness. But except to say that it was murder, the police couldn't say anything else – whether it was gang-related, political or that third thing they say on the news. 'And besides,' the police reporter said, 'there is something else the crime unit was not able to discover, and that's the head.' One of the police theories was that the murder happened in a completely different place and, on the way, when they were moving the dead guy, they lost his head. And that theory even sounds okay, except that Gilad and me know it's wrong. Because when Gilad found him in the bushes, the head was still there. Not actually connected, but in the area. Except that by the time the police got there, Tsuri – who'd been playing basketball with my cousin and was laughing at him for washing his hands in the fountain like some kind of girl because of a little blood and a lizard – just grabbed the head and took off. Gilad didn't actually see him do it, but it's almost a sure thing that's what happened. And to be on the safe side, he didn't say anything to the police about it, because that way, if it really was Tsuri, he wouldn't get the shit beaten out of him afterwards.

Gilad told me that the head had connected eyebrows and a kind of hole in the middle of its chin, like that actor from *Romancing the Stone*, and that the eyes were closed when he saw them, which was very lucky, because if someone without a body zaps a dead person's look on you, you can shit in your pants on the spot. And the last thing a person wants to do next to Tsuri is shit in his pants. Because if Tsuri sees it, within five seconds the whole school knows, including the girls. Gilad's a year older than me, and he's one of the only kids in junior high who has a steady girlfriend, Anat. She goes to a different school. And it's not like they fuck or anything, but still, touching is nothing to sneeze at either. I was dying to have a girl that looked half as good as she did, who'd let me touch her a little, even if only through her clothes. And Gilad says that if there's one thing she likes about him, it's that he knows how to look out for himself, he always sneaks her into the country club pool and stuff like that, so if, let's say, he shit in his pants and she knew, she'd dump him in a second. So he really was lucky. And I thought to myself, what a piece of crap that Tsuri is, stealing the head off a person he doesn't even know like it's a chocolate bar he's swiping from the grocery store. Which is pretty lowdown, because a head without a body is brrr . . . and also because of the person's family, because let's say that man had a kid, then it isn't bad enough he has to see them bury his father, but he also has to think about his head rolling around who knows where, and kids playing ball with it, or smoking and using it as an ashtray. And when we met Tsuri at the shwarma place, I told him so. I told him, 'You think you're funny. But if that was your father and they stole his head, you wouldn't think it was funny at all.' And Tsuri, in the middle of a bite, looked right at me and said, 'You feel like a hero, huh, Shostak? Why, 'cause your hoop star cousin's standing next to you? But even he knows that if you're still here when I finish this pita, his whole meter-fucking-eighty won't help you, and I'll beat the shit out of both of you.' And Gilad said to Tsuri, 'What're you getting so pissed about? It's only Ronny saying what he thinks.' And Tsuri ignored him completely, just bent down to me with his dripping pita and said I better watch my mouth, or else who knows what'll happen.

Gilad and I left, and I didn't say a word. And the man without a head, they never figured out who he was. The police said that they could tell from his prick that he wasn't Jewish, but no one could say who did that to him and why. My father says that in Israel in the old days, a woman could walk down the street alone in the middle of the night and not be afraid of anything, except Arabs maybe. And now it's like America here – people smoking dope and bodies without heads in your kid's schoolyard. And no one even gets excited about it. One day it's in the papers and the next day, no one remembers anything about it. And Mom, who always tries to play things down, told him that maybe everybody's wrong, and the man without a head just killed himself or fell in the dark, and some animal came and took his head. When Dad was talking about it, I thought for a second I'd tell him about Tsuri, but then I remembered how scared Gilad was, and I said to myself, what for? If he's not Jewish, then his kids probably live far away and they won't even know he's dead. And if I tell on Tsuri, I'll just get beat up and ruin things for some kids who live in Romania or Poland who think their father is working now, or living it up in some far-away country.

After summer vacation, I started ninth grade and Gilad's girlfriend was already letting him go all the way. Tsuri dropped out of school and started working in the frozen food locker of the Mega Market, and I got myself a girlfriend too who didn't let me do much of anything, hardly even kiss her. Her name was Merav, and she had the brownest eyes you ever saw in your life, and lips that always looked wet, and a hole in the middle of her chin, just like Gilad said he saw on that man without a head.

HALIBUT

Ever since I came back to Israel, everything looks different to me. Smelly, sad, dull. Even those lunches with Ari that used to light up my day are a drag now. He's going to marry that Nessia of his; today he's going to surprise me with the news. And I, of course, will be surprised, as if Ofer the blinker hadn't told me the secret four days ago. He loves Nessia, he'll say, and look into my eyes. 'This time,' he'll say in his deep and very convincing voice, 'this time, it's real.'

We made a date to meet in a fish place on the beach. The economy's in a recession now, and the price of the lunch specials is a joke, anything so people will come. Ari says the recession is good for us, because we – though we may not have realized it yet – are rich. Recession, Ari explains, is tough on the poor; tough isn't the word – it's a killer. But for the rich? It's like frequent flyer bonus points. You can upgrade all the things you used to do without adding a penny. And just like that, the Johnnie Walker goes from red label to black, and the four-days-plus-half-board turns into a week, anything so people will come, *just come*. 'I hate this country,' I tell him while we're waiting for menus. 'I'd split forever if it weren't for the business.' 'Get serious,' Ari puts his sandalled foot on the chair next to him, 'where else in the world can you find a beach like this?' 'In France,' I tell him, 'in Thailand, in Brazil, in Australia, in the Caribbean . . .' 'Okay, okay, so go,' he interrupts me smugly, 'finish your food, a short espresso and go!' 'I said,' I stress, 'that I'd go if it weren't for the business . . .' 'The business,' Ari bursts out laughing, 'the *business*,' and waves at the waitress for a menu.

The waitress comes over to tell us what the day's specials are, and Ari gives her the disinterested look of someone in love with another girl. 'And for the main dish,' she smiles a natural, irresistible smile, 'we have slices of red tuna in butter and pepper, halibut on a bed of tofu with a teriyaki sauce, and talking fish with salt and lemon.' 'I'll take the halibut,' Ari says quickly. 'What's talking fish?' I ask. 'It's talking fish served raw. It's lightly salted, but not spiced–' 'And it talks?' I interrupt her. 'I highly recommend the halibut,' the waitress continues after a nod, 'I never tried the talking.'

As soon as we started eating, Ari told me about marrying Nessia, or NASDAQ, as he likes to call her. He made up the name when the NASDAQ was still going up and had never bothered to update it. I said congratulations, I'm glad. 'Me too,' Ari slouched a little lower in his seat, 'me too. We have a pretty good life, eh? Me and NASDAQ, you . . . alone, temporarily. A bottle of good white wine, air conditioning, the sea.'

The fish arrived fifteen minutes later; the haibut, according to Ari, was terrific. The talking fish – kept quiet. 'So it doesn't talk,' Ari snapped, 'so what? Jeez, don't start making a scene here. I mean it, I don't have the patience.' And when he saw me still waving to the waitress, he suggested, 'Take a bite – if it's not good, send it back. But at least taste it first.' The waitress came over with the same irresistible smile as before. 'The fish . . .' I said to her. 'Yes?' she asked, craning her already long neck. 'It doesn't talk.' The waitress gave a funny little giggle and explained quickly. 'The dish is called talking fish as an indication of the kind of fish it is, which in this case, is the kind that can talk, but the fact that it can talk doesn't mean that it will at any given moment.' 'I don't understand . . .' I began. 'What is there to understand,' the waitress condescended to me, 'this is a restaurant, not a karaoke club. But if you don't like it, I'd be happy to get you something else . . . you know what? I'd be happy to get you something else anyway . . .' 'I don't want something else,' I insisted pointlessly, 'I want it to talk.' 'It's okay,' Ari cut in, 'you don't have to bring something else. Everything here is great.' The waitress flashed a third identical smile and walked away. And Ari said, 'Man, I'm getting married. Do you get it? I'm marrying the love of my life. And this time . . .' he dropped in a two-second pause, 'this time it's real. This meal, it's a celebration, so come on and fucking eat with me. Without fish and without belly-aching about the country. Just be happy with me, with your good friend, okay?' 'I'm happy,' I said, 'really.' 'So eat that ugly fish already,' he begged. 'No,' I said, and quickly corrected myself, 'not yet.' 'Now, now,' Ari urged, 'now, before it gets cold – or send it back. But not like this. Not with the fish on the table and you not talking . . .' 'It's not getting cold,' I corrected him, 'it's raw. And I don't have to be quiet, we can talk . . .' 'Okay,' said Ari, 'forget it,' and jumped angrily to his feet. 'I've lost my appetite anyway.' He reached for his wallet, but I stopped him. 'Let it be my treat,' I said without getting up, 'in honor of your wedding.' 'Go fuck yourself,' Ari hissed, but let go of his wallet. 'Why do I even try to explain to you about love? You homo. Did I say homo? I wish – asexual –' 'Ari –' I tried to interrupt him. 'Even now,' Ari shook a finger in the air, 'even now I know that later I'll be sorry I said that. But being sorry about it won't make it less true.' 'Mazal tov,' I said, trying to give him one of the waitress' natural smiles, and he gave me a half who-cares, half goodbye wave, and left.

'Is everything all right?' the waitress pantomimed from a distance. I nodded. 'Your check?' she continued her pantomime. I shook my head. I looked at the sea through the glass – a little murky but very powerful. I looked at the fish – lying on its stomach with its eyes closed, its body rising and falling as if it were breathing. I didn't know if this table was for smokers, but I lit up anyway, one of those satisfying 'after' cigarettes. I wasn't really hungry. It was pleasant here, looking out on the sea – too bad there was glass and air conditioning instead of a breeze. I could sit like this looking at the sea for hours. 'Take off,' the fish whispered to me without opening its eyes, 'grab a cab to the airport and hop on the first plane out.' 'But I can't just take off like that,' I explained in a clear, slow voice, 'I have commitments here, business.' The fish shut up again and so did I. Almost a minute later, it added, 'Never mind, forget it. I'm depressed.'

They didn't put the fish on the bill. They offered me dessert instead, and when I said no, they just subtracted forty-five shekels. 'I'm sorry . . .' said the waitress, and quickly explained, 'I'm sorry you didn't enjoy it.' And a second later, she specified, 'the fish'. 'No, no,' I protested, dialing my cell phone for a taxi, 'the fish was good. Really, you have a very nice place here.'

FOR ONLY 9.99 (INC. TAX AND POSTAGE)

Nachum happened on the ad completely by chance, somewhere between the daily horoscope and the sex toys. 'Ever wonder about the meaning of life?' the ad inquired. 'Ever ask yourself why we exist in the first place?' And it went on to provide the solution: 'The answer to this difficult question is right at your fingertips. You'll find it in a small but incredible booklet. In simple and readable language you will find out why you have been placed on this earth. The booklet, printed on the finest paper, complete with enlightening, breathtaking color photographs, will be mailed to your home, beautifully gift-wrapped, for only 9.99!' There was a photograph of a man with glasses reading a small

117

booklet, and smiling happily to himself. And right over his head, in the spot where his thought-bubble should have been, was the inscription, in thick lettering: 'The booklet that will change your life!' Nachum was deeply impressed by the picture in the ad. The man looked very happy, and Nachum was also taken by his broad shoulders, almost like the smiling strongman in the ad for 'The physique of Hercules in only thirty seconds a day, with our new and improved formula. Only 19.99! (inc. tax and postage)'. To think that they were offering him the meaning of life. And at half the price!

Nachum's hands shook as he stuck the stamp on the envelope. He knew that the next few days would be the longest ever. The meaning of life was some-thing that had worried him for as long as he could remember, and even though his life was reasonably pleasant and happy, he'd always felt that there was something missing. But now, in just a few days, his world would be complete. When he tried to explain to his father the intense curiosity that was welling up within him, he encountered some difficulties. 'You're such a moron. Every time some two-timing swindler decides to cash in, all he needs is to place an ad, and my nincompoop of a son sends him the money.' 'But Dad, they're not two-timing swindlers,' Nachum tried to explain. 'The ad even says that if I'm not completely satisfied, I have fourteen days to send the booklet back, and they'll reimburse me. Minus the postage, of course.' Nachum's dad gave a creepy snigger, and his nervous expression became down-right menacing. Placing his hand on Nachum's shoulder, he whispered in a conspiratorial voice: 'Know what? Let's put one over on 'em. Let's read the booklet together, and then, once we've figured out the meaning of life, we'll send it back. That'll screw them good. So whaddya say?' Nachum didn't say anything, though he couldn't help thinking it was very dishonest. He didn't want to upset his dad. But the clamp on his shoulder was growing tighter and tighter. Apparently, his dad had managed to get upset all on his own. 'You imbecile!' he shouted. 'I'll show you the meaning of life, you piece of defective goods,' he ranted on, struggling to pull off his slipper. 'Leave the boy alone,' Nachum's mother rushed to his rescue, trying to separate him from his father. 'Boy?' Nachum's dad wheezed madly, waving the slipper at them like he was about to use it. 'He'll be twenty-eight in August.' 'So he's a bit naive,' his mother whimpered. 'So what?'

Nachum's friends thought it was a scam too. Even Ronit. So, having nobody to share his impatient wait with, he impatiently waited all by himself. The notice from the post office arrived three days later, and Nachum barely managed to grab it from his dad, who was about to swallow it in one of his fits of rage. As soon as he had the package in his hands, even before he'd left the post office, Nachum tore open the brown-paper wrapping and began reading the booklet on his way home. The secret of the human condition was revealed to him, becoming clearer and clearer with every page he read. The incredible booklet was written in such plain and simple language that Nachum could understand everything without having to re-read it (except one part where he had to refer to the breathtaking color photographs, which really were enlightening, just like the ad said). And by the time he got back to the building where he lived, he knew, for the first time in his life, why he had been placed in this wonderful world of ours, why all of us are here. And a feeling of sublime joy swept over him, a joy mingled with just a tinge of sorrow, for all those years that he'd been forced to live in ignorance.

Determined to ensure that others would not have to suffer those tormenting moments of confusion, Nachum raced upstairs, and the very thought that in just a few short seconds he was about to share the secret of the human condition with his parents brought tears to his eyes – tears which were soon to turn into tears of frustration. His father screamed that he would have no part of this ridiculous farce. And while his mother did listen to his explanations, and looked at his pictures and nodded, her eyes were glazed over, and her nod was hollow. Clearly, she wasn't thinking about the booklet at all. She just wanted to make Nachum feel better.

The next few hours left Nachum feeling frustrated and sad. A quick glance at the newspaper was enough to remind him just how foreign the essence of the human condition was to most of humanity. All those wars, and murders, and ecological disasters, even the drops in the stock market – all those things grew out of ignorance, mistakes caused by a basic failure to understand what life was really about. Mistakes which could be corrected so easily, if only they would listen. But nobody was prepared to listen. Not his relatives, not his friends, not even Ronit. With every fiber of his being Nachum felt the disillusionment. But suddenly, just above the array of easy-loan ads, he caught sight of a familiar face – the man with the broad shoulders and the glasses. Except that in this ad he was talking with a stern-looking man who seemed to be listening very closely. 'People don't listen to you?' the ad asked. 'Family and close friends pay no attention? We have the solution. For 9.99 we will send you a remarkable booklet, which will teach you how to win over even the most indifferent listener.' Nachum could hardly contain his joy. Just as he had reached the verge of despair, everything was about to change. The time spent waiting for the booklet was filled with eager

THE NIMROD FLIP-OUT

anticipation, and after four interminable days, he held the package in his hands. With bated breath he read the edifying principles, and when he'd finished, he approached his dad, confident that this time he would listen.

Matters progressed at a dizzying pace. Nachum knew the existential truth, and how to make people listen to him. The meaning of life was passed on by word of mouth, from one friend to another. It's hard to imagine Nachum's elation as he looked into his mother's glistening eyes, or listened to the delighted laughter of all his friends, especially Ronit. But not everything went smoothly. A couple of orthodox kids, including the grandson of the Rabbi of Ludvor, came to visit Nachum at his home, and wanted him to explain the meaning of life to them. Nachum was glad to oblige, and even served them some lemonade. They thanked him politely and left. Nachum didn't give it a second thought. Lots of strangers came to visit him at his home at that point, and those boys were no different.

But the next day hundreds of orthodox people surrounded his home and filled his yard, singing religious hymns like 'Son of Lilith, Fear Our Sword – We Shall Prevail, So Quoth the Lord' and 'Heathens Shall be Smitten'. Listening to their chants, Nachum knew he was in trouble. He managed to sneak out through the bathroom window

122

and to hide in an abandoned shelter not far from his home. Every morning, Ronit would bring him some sandwiches and a thermos of coffee. She'd wrap the sandwiches in newsprint, which is how Nachum discovered that the Rabbi of Ludvor's grandson had organized a mass departure of students from the yeshivas of Jerusalem, on the grounds that there was no point in seeking the truth in the sacred books, now that it was out in the open. The orthodox community held Nachum personally responsible for the whole thing. And as if things weren't bad enough, his father, whose understanding of the meaning of life did not seem to have changed him much, managed to make things even worse. By finding unconventional uses for cans of baby carrots, he had sent the cantor of the Ludvor Congregation to intensive care.

Nachum was keen on making the Chief Rabbi of the Ludvor Congregation realize it was just a misunderstanding, and to explain to him that the meaning of life as he had presented it was devoid of any anti-religious implications. Quite the contrary. He himself, after all, made a point of fasting on Yom Kippur and eating *matzah* every Passover. He'd even received a sports bike for his bar mitzvah like any good Jewish boy. But every time he tried calling the rabbi from the phone booth nearby, the rabbi would just mutter his *Shma Yisrael*, call out for help

123

in Yiddish and hang up before Nachum could say anything. Nachum was growing despondent. He was beginning to feel the effect of the persistent siege on his home and the public denunciation by the rabbis, not to mention the mildew in the shelter and his powerful craving for his mother's cooking. But it was then, just when everything seemed to be going wrong, that it all changed, thanks to Tuesday's tuna fish sandwich. One of the stories in the sandwich wrapping was an interview with the Ludvor cantor, who'd been discharged after making a complete recovery from the canned goods attack, and right above it Nachum spotted an ad. It showed the same broad-shouldered guy, except that this time he was in an awkward position. Right opposite him was a bearded giant, holding a sharp axe, in a menacing pose. The guy with the glasses was giving him a piercing look, reinforced with a dotted line. The ad went like this: 'Do you have any enemies? Anyone who wants to harm you? Don't worry! For 9.99 you can own our new booklet, "Turn Enemies into Friends in Seven Easy Lessons", and learn how to turn negative energies into positive ones with just one look!'

Nachum lost no time sending in his money, and soon the booklet arrived. He read it breathlessly, and began practicing by applying its rules to the misanthropic rats in the shelter. In no time at all, they turned into his friends. Nachum shaved, using the cold water of the shelter, and did his best to iron his clothes. He bought a yarmulke in the nearby used-clothing shop, and set out on his long journey to the residence of the Rabbi of Ludvor. Despite his efforts to maintain a low profile, Nachum, for reasons which were not clear to him, drew a great deal of attention. When he reached the rabbi's residence, the crowd was ready for a lynching, but his friends the rats, who'd followed him around by the dozen, protected him. The rabbi came out onto the balcony to find out what was causing the commotion, and, sure enough, all it took was one look from Nachum to make him realize that there had been a misunderstanding. 'Stop,' he cried from the balcony high above. 'Can't you see that you are facing the Messiah himself, and that he brings us the word of God?' And the crowd looked and could see. That very evening, they held a banquet. Nachum's father and the cantor of Ludvor danced together, arm in arm, as Nachum's rat-friends drank themselves senseless.

It was not long before the meaning of life could be explained to the rest of humanity. The secret of human existence spread like a virus, and Nachum took the trouble to explain it personally on both of his *Nightline* appearances. Every country in the world agreed to disarm, some beating their swords into ploughshares, and others finding even better applications. Nachum spent most of his time growing tomatoes in the little garden he cultivated in the back yard of his parents' apartment building, basking in the knowledge that he, too, had played a role in the happiness of the entire world.

There was just one thought that continued to worry him though: the thought of death. It hadn't bothered him in the past, but now that everything was so wonderful, it horrified him, which is why Nachum was so thrilled when his father drew his attention to an ad in one of the dailies, where the broad-shouldered guy with the glasses, who was looking younger than ever, promised '. . . a colorful booklet that will show you the way to immortality. All you need is fifteen seconds a day of exercising your sphincter muscles. For only 29.99'. 'D'you see that?' Nachum's father grumbled. 'One lucky break, and already they go and up the price.'

HORSIE

'The golden stick' is what they call it, and you have to read the little leaflet that comes with it before your girlfriend pees on it. You make coffee, have a cookie, like everything's cool, watch a clip on MTV, groove on the singer, snuggle, sing the chorus with him. Then back to the stick. The stick has a little window. When there's one stripe in it, that means everything's okay, and when there are two – hell, you always wanted to be a dad anyway.

The truth is, he loved her. But really, not that stammered sure-I-love-you kind of love. He loved her forever, like in the fairytales, I'd-walk-down-the-aisle-tomorrow kind of love, except that the whole business with the baby really stressed him out. It was

127

pretty heavy stuff for her too, but an abortion was even scarier. And if they knew they were heading towards a family anyway, then it was just pushing up the timing a little. 'You're uptight,' she laughed, 'look how you're sweating.' 'Sure I'm uptight,' he tried to laugh too, 'it's easy for you, you have a uterus, but me, you know me, I get uptight even when there's no reason and now that there is . . .' 'I'm scared too,' she wrapped herself around him. 'Forget it,' he hugged her, 'it'll all work out in the end, you'll see. If it's a boy, I'll teach him football, and if it's a girl – you know what, it wouldn't hurt her either.' Then she cried a little and he comforted her, and then she fell asleep and he didn't. Far back, deep inside him, he could feel his haemorrhoids opening one by one like flowers in springtime.

At first, when there was no belly yet, he tried not to think about it, not that it helped, but at least there was something to aim for. Later, when she started showing a little, he began to imagine it sitting there in her stomach, a pocket-sized little asshole in a shiny three-piece suit. And really, how could he know that it wouldn't be born a little shit, because kids, they're like Russian roulette, you never know in advance what you'll get. Once, when she was in her third month, he went to the mall to buy something for his computer and saw a disgusting kid in overalls forcing his mother to buy him a

TV game, pretending he'd haul his chubby little body over the second-floor railing if she didn't. 'Jump,' he shouted at the kid from below, 'I dare you, you little blackmailer', and took off before the hysterical mother could sic the security guards on him. The next night, he dreamed he was pushing his girlfriend down the steps so she'd have a miscarriage. Or maybe it wasn't a dream, just a thought that went through his mind when they went out to the movies, and he started thinking that this was no joke, that he had to do something. Something serious, not on the level of a conversation with his mother or even his grandmother, something that required no less than a visit to his great-grandmother.

His great-grandmother was so old that it wasn't tactful anymore to ask her age, and if there was something she hated, it was visitors. She spent the whole day at home soaking up soap operas, and if she did let someone come to visit, she refused to turn off the TV. 'I'm scared, great-grandmother,' he blubbered on the living room couch, 'I'm so scared, you have no idea.' 'Of what?' the great-grandmother asked, still watching some mustachioed Victor who'd just told a woman wrapped in a towel that he was actually her father. 'I don't know,' he mumbled, 'that something I never wanted will be born.' 'Listen to me carefully, great-grandson,' said the great-grandmother, nodding her head in time to the closing music of the series, 'at night, wait till she falls asleep, and then lie with your head right up against her belly, so that all your dreams move straight into it.' He nodded, even though he didn't really understand, but the great-grandmother explained: 'A dream is really a strong wish. So strong that you can't even put it into words. Now, the fetus, which is in her belly, has no opinions about anything, so he'll sop it right up. Whatever you dream, that's exactly what will be.'

After that, he slept every night with his head right next to her belly, which was getting bigger all the time. He didn't remember the dreams, but was willing to swear they were good ones. And he couldn't remember a time in his life when he'd slept that way, so peaceful like, he didn't even get up to pee. His wife didn't really understand that funny position she found him in every morning, but was happy to see him relaxed again and he stayed relaxed the whole way, right to the delivery room. Not that he didn't care or something, he was very much into it, it was just that his fears had been replaced by anticipation. And even when he saw the obstetrician and the nurses whispering together before the doctor walked over to him reluctantly, not even for a second did he lose his confidence that everything would be fine.

In the end, they had a little horse or, more accurately, a pony. They called him Hemi, after a successful industrialist whose socko TV appearances had impressed the great-grandmother, and they raised him with lots of love. On Saturdays, they rode him to the park and played all kinds of games with him, mainly cowboys and Indians. The truth is that after the birth, she was depressed for a long time, and even though they never talked about it, he knew that no matter how much she loved Hemi, deep in her heart, she wanted something different.

Meanwhile, in the soap opera, the woman in the towel shot Victor, twice, making the great-grandmother very unhappy, and he'd been hooked up to a respirator for quite a few episodes now. At night, after everyone fell asleep, he'd turn off the TV and go to look at Hemi, who slept on the hay he'd spread on the floor of the nursery. Hemi was very funny when he slept, shaking his head from side to side as if he were listening to someone talking to him, and every once in a while he even whinnied because of some especially funny dream. She took him to a lot of specialists, who said he would never really grow. 'He'll stay a midget,' as she'd put it, but Hemi wasn't a midget, he was a pony. 'Too bad,' he'd whisper every night when he put him to sleep, 'too bad Mom couldn't dream a dream that might've come true too,' and then he'd stroke

Hemi's mane and hum him a medley of children's and horses' songs, a medley that always opened with 'All the Pretty Little Ponies' and ended only when he himself fell asleep.

MY GIRLFRIEND'S NAKED

Outside, the sun's shining, and downstairs on the lawn, my girlfriend's naked. June twenty-first, the longest day of the year. People walking past our building look at her, some even find a reason to stop – they have to tie their shoelaces, let's say, or they stepped on some shit and absolutely have to scrape it off their shoes right now. But some of them stop without an excuse, real straight-shooters. Before, one of them even whistled at her, but my girlfriend didn't even notice, because she'd just come to a gripping passage in her book. And the guy who whistled waited for a second, but when he saw her keep on reading, he left. She reads a lot, my girlfriend, but never like that, outside, naked.

And I'm sitting on our balcony on the third floor at the front, trying to figure out how I feel about it. I'm a little strange when it comes to that knowing-how-I-feel thing. Sometimes, friends come over on Saturday night and get all worked up, arguing about all kinds of things. Once, someone even got up in the middle, mad as hell, and went home. And I just sit there with them and watch TV with the sound off and read the subtitles. Sometimes, in the heat of an argument, someone can even ask me what I think. And then, most of the time, I pretend like I'm thinking, finding it hard to put my thoughts into words, and there's always someone who takes advantage of it to jump in with his two cents. But there, we're talking about more general subjects, politics and stuff, and here, this is my girlfriend we're talking about, and she's naked. Really, I tell myself, I should know how I feel about it. Now, the Elizovs come out the front door where the intercom is. The Elizovs live two floors above us, the penthouse. The man's very old, maybe a hundred, I don't even know his first name, just that it starts with an 'S', and that he's an engineer, because next to their regular mailbox there's another one, bigger, that has 'S. Elizov, Engineer', written on it, and it can't be her, because our neighbor across the hall once told me that she's a customs inspector. She's no spring chicken either, Mrs Elizov, and her blonde hair is right out of a bottle. The first time we rode in the elevator with them, my girlfriend was sure she was a call girl because her perfume had a smell kind of like detergent. The Elizovs stop and look at my girlfriend naked on the lawn. They're the two most influential people on the tenants' committee. The climbing vine on the fence, for example, was their idea. Mr Elizov whispers something into his wife's ear, she shrugs, and they keep on walking. My girlfriend doesn't even notice them go past her, she's so caught up in her book, so engrossed. And what I feel, if I really try to put it into words, is that it's great that she gets tan, because when she's tan, it makes the green of her eyes stand out more. And if she's tanning herself anyway, then the best way is naked, because if there's something I hate, it's those bathing suit strap marks, when everything's dark and all of a sudden, white. It always makes you feel that it's not even the same skin, that it's some synthetic thing you buy at Club Med. On the other hand, it's not such a good idea to piss off the Elizovs. Because we're only renting the place and we do have the option to stay for two years, but still. And if they start saying that we're causing problems, the landlord could throw us out with sixty days' notice. It says so in the lease. Even though that on-the-other-hand has nothing to do with anybody's feelings on the subject, definitely not mine, it's more like a kind of risk we have to consider. My girl-friend's turning on her back now. Her ass is my absolute favorite, but her boobs are something too. A kid going by on his rollerblades yells at her, 'Hey, lady, your cunt is showing!' As if she didn't know. My brother once said she's the kind of girl who doesn't stay in one place very long, and I should be pre-pared, so she won't break my heart. That was a long time ago, I think, almost two years. And when that guy down there whistled at her, all of a sudden I remembered that, and for a second I was scared she'd get up and leave.

The sun'll be going down soon, and she'll come back inside. Because there won't be any more light for sunbathing, or for reading either. And when she does come in, I'll slice us some watermelon and we'll eat it on the balcony, together. If it happens real soon, maybe we'll even get to see the sunset.

BOTTLE

Two guys are sitting together in a pub. One of them is majoring in something or other in college, the other abuses his guitar once a day and thinks he's a musician. They've already had two beers, and are planning to have at least two more. The college guy just happens to be depressed, because he's in love with his roommate, and the roommate has a hairy-necked boyfriend who sleeps in their apartment every night, and in the morning, when they accidentally bump into each other in the kitchen, he makes you-have-my-sympathy faces at the college guy, and that only depresses him more. 'Move out,' the guy who thinks he's a musician tells him – this musician guy, he has a history of avoiding conflicts. All of a sudden, in the middle of the conversation, some drunk with a ponytail they've never seen before comes in and asks the college student if he'd bet a hundred shekels that he can put his friend, the musician, into a bottle. The college guy says yes right away, because, really, the bet sounds pretty dumb, and in a second, the ponytail puts the musician into an empty Carlsberg bottle. The college guy doesn't have much money to spare, but fair is fair, he takes out the hundred shekels, pays up, and goes back to staring at the wall and feeling sorry for himself. 'Tell him,' his friend shouts from the bottle. 'Come on, quick, before he goes.' 'Tell him what?' the college guy asks. 'To get me out of the bottle, now, come on!' But by the time the college guy gets the message, the ponytail has split.

So he pays, takes his best friend in the bottle, hails a cab, and together they go looking for the ponytail. One thing's for sure, that ponytail didn't look like someone who got drunk by mistake, he's a pro. So they go from pub to pub. And at each one they have another drink, so they won't feel they came for nothing. The college guy downs them in a single gulp, and the more he drinks, the sorrier he feels for himself. The guy in the bottle drinks through a straw, it's not as if he has too many options.

At five in the morning, when they find the ponytail in a pub near the beach, they're both sloshed. The ponytail is sloshed too, and he feels really bad about the bottle thing. Right away, he says he's sorry, and takes the musician out of the bottle. He's really embarrassed about forgetting the guy inside, so he buys another round for them, their last. They talk a little, and the ponytail tells them that he learned the bottle trick from a Finnish guy he met in Thailand, and it turns out that in Finland that trick is considered kids' stuff. And ever since, every time the ponytail goes out drinking and is stuck without cash, he gets hold of some by betting. And the ponytail even teaches them how to do the trick, that's how bad he feels. The truth? From the minute you catch on, you're amazed at how easy it is.

By the time the college guy gets home, the sun is almost up. And before he can even try to get his key in the lock, the door opens, and there's hairy-neck, standing in front of him, all showered and shaved. Before hairy-neck starts to go down the stairs, he manages to toss his girlfriend's drunk roommate an I-know-you-went-out-to-get-crocked-only-because-of-her look. And the college guy crawls quietly to his room, managing to get a peek at his roommate – Sivan, that's her name – sleeping under the covers in her room with her mouth half open, like a baby. She has this, like, special kind of beauty now, serene. The kind of beauty some people have only when they're sleeping, but not all of them. And for a minute, he feels like taking her, just the way she is, putting her in a bottle and keeping her next to his bed, like those bottles of multicolored sand people used to bring back from the Sinai. Like the small night lights you keep on for kids who are afraid to sleep alone in the dark.

A VISIT TO THE COCKPIT

When we landed in Tel Aviv, the whole airplane applauded and I started to cry. My father, who was sitting in the aisle seat, tried to calm me down, and at the same time to explain to anyone who was polite enough to listen that this was the first time I'd ever flown abroad, and that's why I was a little emotional. 'When we took off, she was actually fine,' he blabbered to an old man with Coke-bottle glasses who stank of piss, 'and now, after landing, all of a sudden she's letting it out.' In the same breath, he put a hand on the back of my neck, the way you do with a dog, and whispered in a syrupy voice, 'Don't cry, sweetie, Daddy's here.' I wanted to kill him, I wanted to hit him so hard that he'd start bleeding. But Daddy kept on kneading the back of my neck, whispering loudly to the smelly old man that I'm not usually like this, and that I'd been an artillery instructor in the army, and that my boyfriend, Giora, how ironic, is even a security officer for El Al.

A week before, when I landed in New York, my boyfriend, Giora, how ironic, was waiting for me with flowers right at the door of the plane. He works at the airport, so arranging it was no problem. We kissed on the steps, like in some corny Hollywood film, and he whisked me and my suitcases through passport control in a second. From the airport, we drove straight to a restaurant that overlooks all of Manhattan. He'd bought an '88 Cadillac, but it was so clean that it looked new. In the restaurant, Giora didn't exactly know what to order, and we finally settled on something with a funny name that looked a little like an octopus and smelled awful. Giora tried to eat it and to say it was good, but after a few seconds, he gave up too, and we both started laughing. He'd grown a beard since I saw him last, and it actually looked good on him.

From the restaurant, we went to the Statue of Liberty and the MOMA, and I pretended to love it, but I had this weird feeling the whole time. I mean, we hadn't seen each other for more than two months, and instead of going to his place and fucking or just sitting and talking a little, we're shlepping around to these tourist attractions that Giora must have seen at least two hundred times, and he's giving me these tired explanations of every single one. In the evening, when we got to his apartment, he said he had a phone call to make, and I went to take a shower. I was still drying myself off, and he'd already cooked a pot of spaghetti and set the table with wine and half-dead flowers. I really wanted us to talk, I don't know, I had this feeling that something bad had happened and he didn't want to tell me, like in those movies when someone dies and they try to hide it from the children. But Giora kept yakking away about all the places he had to show me in a week, about how he was afraid we wouldn't see them all because the city's so big, and it isn't really a week, barely five days, because one day was over already and on the last day, I was flying in the evening, and my father was coming into town before that, so we definitely couldn't do anything. I stopped him with a kiss, I couldn't think of any other way. The bristles of his beard scratched my face a little. 'Giora,' I asked, 'is everything all right?' 'Sure,' he said, 'sure, it's just that we have so little time, and I'm afraid we won't manage to see everything.'

The spaghetti was actually very good, and after we fucked, we sat on the balcony, drank some wine, and looked at all the teeny-tiny people walking down there on the street. I said to Giora that it must be really exciting to live in such a huge city, that I could sit on the balcony like that for hours just watching all those little dots below, trying to guess what they were thinking about. And Giora said, 'No big deal,' and went to get himself a Diet Coke. 'You know,' he said, 'only last night I was about ten blocks east of here, where all the hookers are. You can't see it from here, it's on the other side of the building. And some old homeless guy comes up to the car, he actually looked okay – for a homeless guy. His clothes were old and everything, and he had one of those supermarket carts full of paper bags, the kind they always drag around from place to place; but except for that, he looked completely sane, sort of clean, it's hard to explain. And that homeless guy came up to me and offered to give me a blow job for ten bucks. "I'll do it real good," he said to me, "I'll swallow every drop." And all in a kind of business-like tone, like someone offering to sell you a TV. I didn't know what to do with myself. You know, two in the morning, a line of twenty Puerto Rican hookers standing twenty meters from him, some of them really pretty, and this guy, who looks exactly like my uncle, is offering to give me a blow job. Then it hit him too, it must have been the first time he'd ever offered to do such a thing, and, all of sudden, we were both embarrassed. And he said to me, half apologizing, "So maybe I can wash your car instead? Five bucks. I'm really hungry." And that's how I found myself in the grungiest part of Manhattan, two in the morning, a guy of about forty washing my car with a bottle of mineral water and a rag that used to be a Chicago Bulls T-shirt. Some of the hookers started walking towards us, and a black guy too, who looked like their pimp, and I was sure things were going to get messy, but none of them said a word. They just looked at us without saying anything. And when the guy finished, I said thank you, paid and just drove away.'

Neither of us said anything after that story. I looked at the sky, and it seemed very black all of a sudden. Then I asked him what he was doing on a street of hookers in the middle of the night, and he said that wasn't the point. I asked him if he had someone, and he didn't answer that either. I asked him if she was a hooker. At first, he didn't say anything, then he said she worked for Lufthansa. Now I could suddenly sense her smell on him, coming from his body, his beard. A little like the smell of sauerkraut, and now, after we'd fucked, that smell was clinging to me too. He insisted that I stay in his apartment for the week anyway, and I said yes right away – I didn't have much choice. There was only one bed, and I didn't want to be a bitch, so we slept in it together, but we didn't have sex. I knew I would never fuck him again, and he knew it too. After he fell asleep, I went to take another shower, to wash her smell off me, even though I knew that as long I slept in the same bed with him, the smell would remain.

On the day of the flight, I wore my nicest clothes so Giora would get a little taste of what he was missing, but I don't think he even noticed. I was really happy when we went to meet my father at the hotel. I gave him a big hug, and that surprised him a little, but you could see how happy he was. My father asked Giora a few stupid questions, and Giora squirmed a little, saying he had something urgent to take care of, and he was sorry he couldn't drive us to the airport. Then he went to get my suitcases from the car and as we said goodbye and pretended to kiss, my father couldn't tell anything was wrong. When Giora was gone, I went up to my father's room and showered again, and my father called for a cab to take us to the airport.

During the flight, I was very quiet, and he talked the whole time. That week had passed so slowly for me, and to cheer myself up, I'd tell myself it was the last time I'd spend that day of the week there, just like I did in the last week of basic training, only this time it didn't really help. And even now, with the nightmare finally over, I didn't feel any relief. Even the smell of her was still there. I sniffed myself, trying to figure out where it was coming from, and suddenly I realized it was from my watch. Her smell had stayed on my watch from the very first night.

After the meal, my father pretended he was going to the bathroom and came back with a flight attendant. That's when it dawned on me that he'd arranged a surprise visit to the cockpit for me. I was such a wreck that I didn't even have the strength to argue with him. I dragged myself behind the flight attendant to the cockpit, where the pilot and the navigator explained all kinds of boring things to me about the instruments and the switches. Finally, the pilot, who had gray hair, asked how old I was, and the navigator burst out laughing. The pilot gave him a murderous look, and he stopped and apologized. 'I didn't mean anything,' he said. 'I'm just used to, you know, mostly kids coming in here.' The pilot said that, in any case, it was very nice of me to visit them in the cockpit, and asked if I'd had a good time in New York. I said yes. The pilot said he was crazy about that city, because it had everything. And the navigator, who probably felt a little uncomfortable and wanted to say something too, said that he personally had a little problem with the poverty you see there, but today, with all the Russian immigrants, you actually see it in Israel too. After that, they asked me if I'd gotten to eat in that new restaurant that overlooks all of Manhattan, and I said yes.

When I went back, my father was beaming and he changed places with me so I could see the landing better. As I tried to push my seat into a reclining position, he rubbed the back of my hand and said, 'Sweetie, the red light's on, you'd better fasten your safety belt, we're going to land in a jiffy.' And I fastened my safety belt real tight and felt how, in a jiffy, I was going to cry.

A THOUGHT IN THE SHAPE
OF A STORY

This is a story about people who once
lived on the moon. Nowadays, there's no one up
there, but until not too many years ago, the place
was packed. The people on the moon thought they
were very special, because they could think their
thoughts in any shape they wanted. In the shape of
a pot, or a table, even in the shape of flared pants.
So people on the moon could bring their girlfriend
an original present, like an I-love-you thought in
the shape of a coffee mug or an I'll-always-be-true
thought in the shape of a vase.

It was very impressive, all those shaped thoughts,
except that as time passed, the people on the moon
came to a kind of agreement about how every

thought should look. A mother-love thought should always be shaped like a curtain, while a father-love thought was shaped like an ashtray, so that it didn't matter what house you walked into, you could always guess what thoughts in what shape would be waiting there arranged on the tea trolley in the living room.

Of all the people on the moon, there was one who shaped his thoughts differently. He was a young guy, a little strange, and most of the time he was troubled by existential, slightly irritating questions. The main thought that kept going through his mind was the kind that believes that every person has at least one unique thought that resembles only itself and him. A thought with color and volume and content that only that person could have.

That guy's dream was to build a spaceship, sail around space in it and collect all the unique thoughts. He didn't go to social events, he hardly went out at all, he just spent all his time building the spaceship. He built the engine in the shape of a thought of wonder, and the steering system in the shape of a thought of pure logic, and that was only the beginning. He added lots of other sophisticated thoughts that would help him navigate and survive in outer space. But his neighbors, who watched him while he worked, saw that he was constantly making mistakes. Because only someone who really had no idea could create a thought of curiosity in the shape of an engine, when it was absolutely clear that a thought like that had to look like a microscope. Not to mention that a thought of pure logic, if you don't want it to look tacky, has to be shaped like a shelf. They tried to explain it to him, but he just didn't listen. His desire to find all the true thoughts in the universe went beyond the bounds of good taste, not to mention sanity.

One night, when the young guy was sleeping, a few of his neighbors on the moon got together and, because they felt sorry for him, they went to the spaceship, which was almost finished, and took it apart, thought by thought, and rearranged it. When the young guy got up in the morning, he found shelves, vases, thermoses and microscopes where his spaceship had been. The whole pile was covered with a thought of sorrow – in the shape of an embroidered tablecloth – about his beloved dog that had died.

The young guy was not at all happy about the surprise. And instead of saying thank you, he went crazy, started carrying on and breaking things. The people on the moon watched him, stunned. They really did not like that sort of misbehavior. The moon, as you know, is a star with very little gravitational force. And the smaller a star's gravitational force is, the more dependent it is on discipline and order, because it takes only a little push for objects to lose their equilibrium. And if everyone who felt a little bitter started carrying on, it would simply end in disaster. In the end, when they saw that the young guy was not going to cool down, they had no choice but to think of a way to stop him. So they thought one thought of loneliness that was about three by three, and put him inside it, a thought the size of a cell with a very low ceiling. And every time he accidentally touched one of the sides, he felt a kind of cold blast that reminded him that he was alone.

It was in that cell that he thought a last thought of despair in the shape of a rope, made a noose and hanged himself. The people on the moon were so excited about the idea of a rope of despair with a noose on one end that they immediately thought despair thoughts of their own and wound them around their necks. And that's how all the people on the moon became extinct, leaving behind only that cell of loneliness. But after a hundred years of space storms, it collapsed too.

When the first spaceship reached the moon, the astronauts didn't find anyone. What they did find were a million craters. At first, the astronauts thought those craters were ancient graves of people who had once lived on the moon. Only when they looked closely did they discover that those craters were just thoughts about nothing.

GUR'S THEORY OF
BOREDOM

Of all my friends, my friend Gur has the most theories. And of all his theories, the one that definitely has the best chance of being right is his theory of boredom. Gur's theory of boredom claims that everything that happens in the world today is because of boredom: love, war, inventions, fake fireplaces – ninety-five per cent of all that is pure boredom. He includes in the other five per cent, for example, the time two black guys beat the hell out of him when they robbed him on the subway in New York two years ago. Not that those two guys weren't a little bored, but they looked a lot more hungry than anything else. He likes to explain this whole theory of his at the beach, when he's too tired to play paddle ball or go into the water. And I sit and listen for the thousandth time, secretly hoping that this is the day a babe'll show up. Not that we'd try to hit on her or anything, just for the hell of it, so there'd be something to look at.

The last time I heard Gur's theory was a week ago, when some plainclothes cop caught us on Ben Yehuda Street with a shoebox full of grass. 'Most laws come from boredom, too,' Gur explained to them on the way in the patrol car, 'and that's really cool, because it makes things interesting. People who break the law are uptight about getting caught, and that helps them pass the time. And the police – the police really have a ball. Because everyone knows that when you're enforcing the law, time flies. That's why, in principle, I have no problem with your arresting us. There's only one thing I have a little trouble understanding, why the handcuffs?'

'Shut your face,' barked the plainclothes cop with the sunglasses sitting in the back with us. You could tell he wasn't too thrilled about having to go into the station with two fuck-ups who smoke grass, instead of with some serial rapist or terrorist, or even just an everyday bankrobber.

Gur and me really dug the interrogation, because not only was there an air conditioner, but there was also a cute lady cop who sat with us for a few hours, who even made us some coffee in Styrofoam cups, and Gur explained his theory on the war between the sexes to her, and managed to make her laugh at least twice. In fact, it was all very laid back, except for one slightly scary thing, when a cop who'd seen too many *NYPD Blue* episodes came into the room in the middle and wanted to slap us around. But we played it smart and confessed to everything before he could even get close to us.

Now, when I tell only the interesting parts, it probably sounds as if it all happened very fast, but the truth is that by the time that whole business with the forms was over, it was night-time. Gur called Orit, who'd been his girlfriend for almost eight straight years, and didn't wise up enough to leave him until six months earlier and find herself a boyfriend who was more together. She came right down to the station to post our bail. She came alone, without her boyfriend, making like this was just another load Gur was dumping on her, and she was really so pissed off. But the truth was, you could tell she was happy to see him and she'd really missed him. After she sprang us, Gur wanted to go have coffee or something with her, but she said she had to run, because she was working the night shift at the Super-Pharm, and maybe another time. And Gur told her that he'd been calling her a lot and leaving her messages of love, but she never called him back, and if he hadn't

155

been arrested, he never would've seen her at all, and she told him it would be better if he didn't call, because nothing good would ever come of their being together, or of him either, as long as he kept hanging out with guys like me and did nothing but eat shwarma, smoke joints and eyeball girls. And I didn't get put out when she talked that way about me, because there was something really friendly about it, and besides, it was true. 'I really am late,' she said, and got into her Beetle. And as she'd pulled away, she even waved goodbye through the window.

Then we walked all the way home from the police station on Dizengoff Street without talking, which is pretty normal for me but really unusual for Gur. 'Tell me,' I said to him when we reached my block, 'that boyfriend of Orit's, you want us to beat the shit out of him?' 'Forget it,' Gur mumbled, 'he's an okay guy.' 'I know,' I told him, 'but still, if you want, we can beat the shit out of him.' 'No,' Gur said, 'but I think I'll take your bike now and ride over to look at Orit for a while at the Super-Pharm.' 'Sure,' I said, and gave him the key.

That was one of his regular pastimes, going to look at Orit when she worked nights. And, honestly, if you look at it theoretically, hiding behind a bush for five hours to watch someone ring things up on a cash register and put aspirin and Q-Tips in bags really is something you do out of boredom, except somehow, when it came to Orit, those theories of Gur's never seemed to work.

THE TITS OF AN
EIGHTEEN-YEAR-OLD

'There's nothin' like the tits of an eighteen-year-old,' the cab driver said, and honked at one who was naive enough to turn around. 'Believe me, you sink your teeth into one or two of those a day, and your bald spot disappears,' then he laughed and touched the place on his head where he once had hair. 'Don't get me wrong. Me, I got two kids that age. And if I ever caught my daughter with some old fart my age – I don't know what I'd do to her. But that's the way it is, that's nature, that's how God created us, right? So tell me, why should I be ashamed? There, look at that one,' he honked at a girl with a Walkman who didn't turn around. 'How old would you say she was? Sixteen? And look

159

at that ass. Tell me the truth, wouldn't you like a piece of that?' He honked another few times before giving up, 'Doesn't hear a thing, that one,' he explained, 'because of the tape. I'm tellin' you, after you see one like that, how can you go back to your wife.' 'You're married?' I asked, trying to sound accusing. 'Divorced,' the driver mumbled and tried to keep a little more of the girl with the Walkman in the rearview mirror. 'Believe me, how can you even think about goin' back to the wife.' There was a sad song on the radio, and the driver, who was trying to sing along with it, was too happy to stick with that kind of beat. He switched to a different station, where another sad song was waiting. 'It's because of all that shit with the helicopters,' he explained to me, as if I'd just landed from Mars, 'those helicopters that crashed in mid-air. Didya hear about it? They announced it before, on the news.' I nodded. 'Now they're gonna kill our shifts for us. I swear, nothin' but bad news and sad songs.' At a pedestrian crossing, he stopped for a tall young girl wearing a back brace. 'She's not bad either, huh?' he said, hesitating a little. 'Give her maybe another year or two,' and then he honked at her too, just to be on the safe side. He kept switching radio stations, and stopped on one that was reporting from the site of the crash. 'Take me, for example,' he said, 'I got a kid in the army now, in a combat unit. Haven't heard from him in two days. So if I say you gotta put somethin' lighter on the radio when these disasters happen, nobody would say I was wrong, right? What I'm sayin' is, they're gettin' us all worked up for nothin'. Think about his mother, my ex, she gotta listen to all those songs about soldiers whining 'cause their buddy died in their arms, instead of somethin' to take the edge off. Come on,' he suddenly touched my hand, 'let's call her, yank her chain a little.' I didn't answer, slightly taken aback when he touched me. 'Hey, Rona, howya doin'?' he was already yelling into the speaker phone. 'Everythin' okay?' He winked at me and gestured towards a peroxide in a beat-up Subaru Justy standing next to us at the light. 'I'm worried about Yossi,' a slightly metallic voice replied from the other end, 'he didn't call.' 'How can he call? He's in the army, in the field. Whaddya think, they got payphones on the front?' 'I don't know,' the woman said, 'I have a bad feeling.' 'You're really somethin', you and your feelings,' the driver winked at me again. 'I'm just sayin' to this passenger here that, if I know you, you're worryin'.' 'Why, you aren't?' 'No,' the driver laughed, 'and you know why? Because I'm not like you, I listen to what they actually say on the radio, not only to those tearjerkers in the middle. And what they say is that the ones in the helicopters were paratroopers, and our Yossi isn't a paratrooper, so whaddya got to worry about?' 'They said *also* paratroopers,' Rona mumbled, 'that doesn't mean there weren't others.' Even though the connection was bad, I could hear her crying. 'Do me a favor, there's this open line for parents. Call them and ask about him. Come on, for me.' 'Didn't I just tell you,' the driver insisted, 'they said only paratroopers. I'm not gonna call now and make a schmuck outta myself.' And when he didn't get an answer from the other end, he went on: 'You wanna look like a retard? So you call.' 'Okay,' she tried to sound tough. 'So get off the line.' 'Well listen to you!' the driver said, and hung up. 'Now she'll even spend ten hours tryin' to get them, anything, just so they check it for her.' He gave a short, empty laugh. 'Real stubborn, that one, don't listen to no one.' He was looking through the windshield for something to honk at, but the streets were almost deserted. 'Believe me,' he said, 'an ugly young girl is better than a beautiful old broad, and I'm talkin' from experience. A young one, even if she's ugly, her skin's still tight, her tits stand up, her body has a kinda smell, young. I'm tellin' you, there are lots of beautiful things in the world, but the body of a seventeen-, eighteen-year-old girl . . .' He tried to hum a different song from the one on the radio, and after two verses, the car phone rang. 'That's her,' he smiled at me and winked again. 'Rona honey,' he moved his face closer to the speaker phone, as if he were a radio broadcaster flirting with his listeners, 'how are you?' 'Fine,' the woman answered in a happy voice, making an effort to sound formal. 'I just called to tell you they said he's okay.' 'Is that what you're callin' for?' the driver laughed. 'You dummy, I already told you fifteen minutes ago he was okay, didn't I?' 'You did,' she sighed, 'but now I feel better.' 'So good for you,' he tried to be sarcastic. 'Okay, I'm going to sleep, I'm dead tired.' 'Sweet dreams,' the driver put his finger on the button that disconnects the car phone, 'and next time, listen to me, huh?' We were very close to my house now, and pulling into Reiness Street he saw a thin girl in a mini skirt who turned around, frightened, when he honked. 'Get a loada that one,' he said, trying to hide his tears. 'Say, wouldn't you like to stick it to her?'

BWOKEN

For Yaniv he brought a toy monkey wearing a peaked cap. When you pressed the monkey's back, it made a strange growling sound, stuck out a long tongue that reached its nose, and crossed its eyes. Dafna thought it was an ugly toy and that Yaniv would be afraid of it. But Yaniv actually seemed delighted. 'Huaaah!' he'd try to imitate the monkey's growl. He couldn't cross his eyes, so he blinked instead, and then laughed with pleasure. There's something so perfect about a child's enjoyment that nothing can compete with it. And in Daddy-Avner's present state of mind, he couldn't really compete with slightly less perfect enjoyment either.

For Dafna he brought some perfume from the duty-free shop – she'd written the name on a piece of paper for him. There'd been a small bottle and a large one, and he bought the large one without hesitating – when it came to money, Husband-Avner was never stingy. 'I asked for eau-de-toilette,' Dafna said, 'that's what my note said.' 'And . . .?' he asked impatiently. 'It doesn't matter,' Dafna smiled a bitter smile that said exactly the opposite, 'you bought perfume. It's a drop too strong on me, but it's great too.'

For his mother, he brought a carton of Kent Longs. His mother was easy when it came to gifts. 'I want you to know that I'm very worried about Yaniv,' she said, ripping the cellophane wrapper off the carton of cigarettes. 'What's wrong with Yaniv?' Son-Avner asked in the indifferent tone of someone who knows who he's dealing with. 'At the pediatric clinic they said he's short for his age and when he gets hit, he doesn't hit back, but that's not –' 'What do you mean, "When he gets hit"? Somebody hit him?' 'I hit him, a little, not really hit, push, to teach him to defend himself. But all he does is curl up in a corner and scream. I'm telling you, next year he's going to nursery school, and if he doesn't learn how to defend himself by then, the other children will make chopped meat out of him.' 'No one will make anything out of him,' he got angry, 'and

you, stop being a hysterical grandmother.' 'All
right, all right,' his mother pouted and lit a
cigarette, 'but if you'd let me finish, you would've
heard that I said myself that wasn't the half of it.
What I really find hard to take is that the child
doesn't know how to say "Daddy". Did you ever
hear of a child who doesn't know how to say
"Daddy"? And it's not that he doesn't talk. He
knows lots of words – "cookie", "baby", "cat", you
name it, only "Daddy" he doesn't know, and if it
weren't for me, he wouldn't have learned "Nana"
either.' 'He doesn't call me "Daddy", he calls me by
a nickname instead,' he tried to smile. 'You don't
have to blow it all out of proportion.' 'Excuse me,
Avner, but "Hello!" is not a nickname. "Hello!" is
what you shout into the phone when you can't hear.
You know, he calls Aviv, your downstairs neighbor,
by his name, but when it comes to his own father,
he yells "Hello!". Like you're some hooligan who
grabbed his parking spot.'

'This country is like a woman,' Businessman-
Avner said to the German investor in labored
English, 'beautiful, dangerous, unpredictable –
that's part of its magic. I wouldn't exchange it for
any other place in the world.' As often happened to
him, he wasn't certain if what he was saying was
really true, maybe it was, but one thing was for sure,
it worked much better with investors than the other

kinds of thoughts, the frightening ones that go through his mind. 'This country is the black under the fingernails of the Western world – thinks it's Europe, but it's nothing more than a lump of sweat and dirt that's developed a consciousness.' No, words like those don't earn you dividends. 'Now, tell me the truth, Herman,' he smiled and handed his credit card to the tastefully tattooed waitress, 'is there anyplace in that Frankfurt of yours that makes such good sushi?'

After he came, they stayed in the same position. She was kneeling on all fours and he was bending over her. They didn't move, and they didn't say anything either, as if they were afraid of spoiling this good thing that had happened by some fluke. When he got tired, he leaned his head on her shoulder and closed his eyes. 'We're good,' Dafna whispered, as if to herself, but actually for him. And he felt cheated. Let her say she's good, Lover-Avner thought, why does she insist on dragging me into it too, taking over, calling it by name. His eyes stayed closed; he could feel her slide out from under his body, and himself sinking into the mattress. 'We're good together,' she took the trouble to specify, and ran her hand along his spine in a half-medical movement, as if measuring the distance between his brainstem and the tip of his prick. He kept on digging into the mattress. 'Say something,' she whispered in his ear. 'What?' he asked. 'It doesn't matter,' she whispered, 'anything.' 'Don't you think it's strange that he doesn't know how to say "Daddy"?' he asked, turning his gaze to her. 'You know, he can even say "apple" already, and the names of half the people in the building.' 'I don't think it's strange at all,' Dafna went back to her regular, businesslike voice. 'He calls you "Hello!" and you come – so he thinks your name is "Hello!". If it bothers you, correct him.' 'It doesn't really bother me,' he muttered, 'I'm just wondering if it's normal.'

In the evening, Spectator-Avner sat in front of the TV and watched Yaniv, who was playing with his toy monkey which, for some reason, had stopped growling. 'Hello!' Yaniv shouted at him, waving the toy monkey. 'Hello!' 'Daddy,' Daddy-Avner whispered pleadingly, his voice almost inaudible. 'Hello!' Yaniv insisted, shaking the monkey violently. 'Bwoken!' 'Say "Daddy" and I'll fix it,' Businessman-Avner said with surprising sharpness. 'Hello!' Yaniv yelled, 'Hel-l-l-o-o-o! Bwo-o-o-ken!' 'It's up to you,' Avner didn't cave in, 'either "Hello!" and "Bwoken", or "Daddy" and "Huaaah"!' Yaniv listened to Businessman-Avner imitating the monkey's growl, froze for an instant, then burst out laughing. At first, Person-Avner thought the laughter was scornful, but a minute later he could see that it was nothing more than true happiness. 'Huaaah!' Yaniv

169

laughed, left the toy monkey on the floor and began walking towards him in determined, though not altogether steady steps. 'Huaaah! Hello!' 'Huaaah!' Daddy-Hello growled, and swung the laughing Yaniv in the air, 'Huaaaaah!'

BABY

On his twenty-ninth birthday, there was a cool breeze at the beach, and he knew it. True, he was nowhere near it, because she hated sand and water, but still he knew. There's always a cool breeze at the beach. They were in a cab coming back from somewhere, and he clutched the cardboard box wrapped in birthday paper the whole way. That present, in the cardboard box, was the biggest present he'd ever received. Not the most beautiful, but definitely the biggest. And he kept his arm around her the whole way, kissed her on the cheek, the breasts, more surprised with every kiss that she wasn't embarrassed. When he paid him, the ugly driver said he'd never seen a more perfect couple. He's on the road a lot, circling the city like a vulture over an open grave, but he's never seen a couple like them. And the second the driver said that, he felt this heat in his body. A buried heat that only spread on the rare occasions when a great truth is in the air. And when he told her later, in bed, how he'd felt at that moment, she said that if he needed positive reinforcement from a pimple-faced cab driver who couldn't even stay in his own lane, then their relationship must really be over. He pressed up against her and said she had such a nice heart and he loved it. She cried like a princess and said she wanted him to love her, all of her, not just her organs. Their eyes were closing now, and the sea breeze cooled his face as he fell asleep beside her, curled into himself like a child, like a baby.

IRONCLAD RULES

    Usually, we don't kiss around other people. Cecile, with her plunging necklines and fuck-me shoes is actually very shy. And I'm one of those guys who's always aware of every movement around him, who never manages to forget where he is. But it's a fact that on that morning, I did manage to forget, and we suddenly found ourselves, Cecile and me, hugging and kissing at a table in a coffee house like a pair of high school kids trying to steal themselves a little intimacy in a public place.

When Cecile went to the bathroom, I finished my coffee in one gulp. I used the rest of the time to straighten out my clothes and my thoughts. 'You're a lucky guy,' I heard a voice with a thick Texas accent say from very close by. I turned my head. At the next table was an older guy wearing a baseball cap. The whole time we were kissing, he was sitting practically on top of us, and we'd been rubbing and moaning into his bacon and eggs without even noticing. It was very embarrassing, but there was no way of apologizing without making it worse. So I gave him a sheepish smile and nodded.

'No, really,' the old guy went on, 'it's rare to hold on to that after you're married. A lot of people get hitched and it just disappears.' 'Like you said,' I kept on smiling, 'I'm a lucky guy.' 'Me too,' the old guy laughed and raised his hand in the air, to show me his wedding band. 'Me too. Forty-two years we're together, and it isn't even starting to get boring. You know, in my work, I have to fly a lot, and every time I leave her, let me tell you, I just feel like crying.' 'Forty-two years,' I gave a long, polite whistle, 'she must really be something.' 'Yes,' the old guy nodded. I could see that he was trying to make up his mind whether to pull out a picture or not, and I was relieved when he gave up on the idea. It was getting more embarrassing by the minute, even though he clearly had good intentions. 'I have three rules,' the old guy smiled, 'three ironclad rules that help me keep it alive. You want to hear them?' 'Sure,' I said, gesturing at the waitress for more coffee. 'One,' the old guy waved a finger in the air, 'every day I try to find one new thing I love about her, even the smallest thing, you know, the way she answers the phone, how her voice rises when she's pretending she doesn't know what I'm talking about, things like that.' 'Every day?' I said. 'That must really be hard.' 'Not that hard,' the old guy laughed, 'not after you get the hang of it. The second rule – every time I see the children, and now the grandchildren too, I say to myself that half of my love for them is actually for her. Because half of them is her. And the last rule –' he continued as Cecile sat down next to me, 'when I come back from a trip, I always bring my wife a present. Even if I only go for a day.' I nodded again and promised to remember that. Cecile looked at us a little confused; after all, I wasn't exactly the kind of person who starts conversations with people in public places, and the old guy, who'd probably realized that, got up to leave. He touched his hat and said to me, 'Keep it up.' And then he gave Cecile a small bow and left. ' "My wife"?' Cecile grinned and made a face. ' "Keep it up"?' 'It was nothing,' I stroked her hand, 'he saw my wedding band.' 'Ah,' Cecile kissed me on the cheek. 'He looked a little weird.'

On the flight back home, I sat alone, three seats all to myself, but as usual I couldn't fall asleep. I was thinking about the deal with the Swiss company, which I didn't actually think would get off the ground, and about that PlayStation I bought for Roy with the cordless joystick and everything. And when I thought about Roy, I kept trying to remember that half of my love for him is actually for Mira, and then I tried to think about one small thing I love about her – her expression, trying to stay cool, when she catches me in a lie. I even bought her a present from the duty-free cart in the plane, a new French perfume, which the smiling young flight attendant had said everyone was buying now and even she herself was using it. 'Tell me,' the flight attendant said, extending the back of her bronzed hand towards me, 'isn't that a fantastic scent?' Her hand really did smell great.

A GOOD-LOOKING

COUPLE

I have nothing to lose, the girl thought, helping him open her bra with one hand, leaning on the doorframe with the other. If he's a lousy fuck, I can at least say I had a lousy fuck, and if he's a great fuck, well that's even better; I'll enjoy it, plus I'll be able to say I had a great fuck, or if he's shitty to me afterwards, I can say he was a lousy fuck just to get back at him.

I have nothing to lose, the guy thought. If she's a good fuck, I got lucky, and if she gives me a blow job, that's even better – but even if she's a lousy fuck, she's still one more girl. The twenty-second. The twenty-third, actually, if you count a hand job.

Something's going on, the cat thought, people

coming in, bumping into furniture, making a racket, it's that kind of night. A lot of noise, but no milk for a long time, and hardly any food in the bowl, and even the little bit that's left is gross. That cat on the outside of the empty can might be smiling, but me, after licking the inside, I know he has nothing to smile about.

I'm optimistic, the girl thought, he's got a nice touch, kind of soft, maybe this really is the beginning of something, maybe this is love. It's hard to know about things like that. I once had someone like him who turned into a real affair, but even that bombed out in the end. He was nice, but egocentric, nice to himself, mostly.

I'm optimistic, the guy thought, if we got this far, she probably won't stop in the middle, even though, who knows, I've met a few of those too. And then those impossible conversations. Sitting for hours in the living room, when you get into that sincerity routine, like there's something really deep going on. On the other hand, even that's better than the alternative. Especially when it's watching TV and eating baked beans.

I've had it, the TV thought, I've had it with how they turn me on and then leave the room, with how they sit in front of me but don't really watch. If they'd only take the trouble, they'd find out that I have so much to offer, a lot more than sports and clips and news; but for that, they have to dig a little deeper. And they stare at me like I was some piece of ass; if there's a cool clip or some goal on the scoreboard, then great, and if not, they're gone.

It's cold, the cat thought, too cold. Three weeks ago there was still sun, I'd sit outside on the air conditioner, happy as a king, and now I'm freezing, and them, they're warming each other up, having a ball, what do they care if it's cold here at night, and during the day, only noise, and soot. Personally, I've had it with this country.

Why am I always so cynical, the girl thought, why do I have to keep thinking all the time instead of just enjoying myself, looking at him through the slits of my eyes, and caring only what he thinks of me?

Wait, better not come too fast, the guy thought, it's not as much fun and it's uncool too, and she looks like the type who'll go and talk about it if you piss her off. There are techniques, I once heard something about it, maybe if I try to enjoy it less, be a little out of it, it'll take longer.

He locked me, the door thought. Twice. From the inside. Most of the time he leaves me open, maybe it's the visitor. Maybe he locked me without thinking, because in his heart, he wanted her to stay. She actually looks like a nice person, a little sad, a little untrusting, but nice. The kind that, if you just uncover the manhole, everything inside is full of honey.

I'd get up to go to the bathroom, the girl thought, but I'm scared. The floor looks a little sticky. A guy's apartment, what can you do. And if I start getting dressed now just for those few steps, I'll look like some kind of nutcase or retard. I don't want that. Absolutely not. No way.

I could really be somebody, the guy thought, somebody great, a winner. I have things to say, but somehow I can't manage to say them. Maybe she'll understand.

I think I'll meow now, the cat thought. What do I have to lose? Maybe they'll notice me, pet me a little, fill the bowl with milk. Girls like cats, I know, from experience.

What a good-looking couple, the door thought. I'd really be happy if something came of it, if they moved in together. This place could definitely use a woman's touch.

I was uptight for no reason, the woman thought. The floor's even cleaner than mine, and the bathroom too. And his eyes, they're good eyes, and he kept holding me even after he came. I don't know if anything'll come of it, but even if it ends here, it was nice.

Maybe if I played an instrument, the guy thought, if I'd stuck to it when I was a kid. Sometimes, there are these melodies in my head. It's so cute, the way she walks, tiptoeing, like she's afraid the floor's dirty. It's a good thing the maid was here on Friday.

A good program's starting on me now, the TV thought, now, of all times, when there's no one to watch. It pisses me off. Worse than pisses me off. If only I wasn't on mute, I could yell.

ANGLE

There's no telling why the three of them called it snooker when the game is actually called pool. But the truth is it isn't the name that counts, what counts is the pastime. And this way they could meet every day by the billiard table at the café, set up some kind of mini-tournament and feel like they were doing something. Most of the time, the games were pretty evenly balanced, because the only one who had a bit of experience, on account of growing up in the projects, was uncoordinated. The second guy may have had pretty good coordination, but he wasn't really motivated. And the third one, who was motivated as hell, didn't have an angle. Which meant that every time it was his turn, his shot was so impossible that he didn't stand a chance, even in theory.

Pool is a game for two, so that one of them would always have to sit it out, drinking coffee and talking on his mobile. The one who'd grown up in the projects would phone his girlfriend and talk baby-talk to her on his mobile, rubbing his finger around the plastic part that you speak into as if he was stroking her lips. It's amazing how people can sound like retards when they're talking to their girlfriend, especially if they really love her a lot. Because when you're just fucking someone you make a point of keeping your cool, but when you're really in love – it can sound pretty repulsive. Speaking of fucking, the other guy, the one with the good coordination, he never took a latté, just a short and mean espresso, and meanwhile he'd be trying to navigate between all the calls from girls he'd come on to in the past week, putting one on hold, talking to another, on like that. And he put so much effort into making sure that none of the relationships he was juggling got too serious, that none of them ever did. Which sometimes, from a distance, seemed kind of sad.

And the third guy, the motivated one, was the only one who didn't order anything, and hardly ever used his mobile, that's how immersed he was in the game. Once, he even tried to make a rule that whenever they played, they would switch off their mobiles, but the others refused, which was sort of frustrating, because they were so busy wheeling and dealing that they never gave their all to the game. Sitting on the side, instead of drinking and talking, he spent most of his time hating himself for losing the previous round. And somehow, it was always the same story, that when it came time for the critical shot, he didn't have an angle. The truth is that he didn't often sit it out, because he was so into it that whenever he had a miss, he'd start cheating. And the others would almost always let him get away with it, because when you drag it out with the same girl-friend for three years, or when there are four chicks that you're feeling bad about, all at the same time, then losing a game of snooker starts to seem like small change. So that, on paper, everything should have just kept going. Except that the motivated guy knew in his heart that if he wanted to win, he'd have to keep cheating, and that he was cheating his best buddies. And it bothered him, because deep down inside he was a very honest guy. And he was so set on finding a different solution that he'd stay behind every day after his buddies left to practice, trying to figure out what he was doing wrong. From the side, it looked sort of pathetic: a bald thirty-two-year-old kid racking up the balls, shooting with the tip of the cue, and cursing himself almost voicelessly every time he missed.

It went on that way for many days till the waitress who worked there decided to help him. She taught him one simple trick: always, a tenth of a second before you shoot, you should stop thinking about the shot, and think about something else instead, something nice. Surprisingly, this trick almost always worked, and suddenly he became so good that his friends didn't want to play with him any more. They both said that was the reason, but the truth was that there were other reasons. The guy from projects was about to become a father, and he was busy all the time with ultrasounds and mortgages and all kinds of Lamaze courses. And the other guy had so many girls and bad scenes on his mind that he couldn't concentrate long enough to hold the cue straight. So the only thing left for the motivated guy was to play against the waitress. And even though she'd beat him all the time, he didn't really care anymore. This waitress was called Karen, and she had one ironclad rule – not to date customers – but because the motivated guy never ordered anything, she didn't really consider him a customer, so at least in theory he stood a chance.

HIMME

At age thirty-one, Himme found that almost all the dreams the people closest to him ever had for him were coming true: He'd succeeded no less than everyone had expected him to, but he remained modest, which made his father proud. Not to mention the fact that he had married just the way his parents and his wife had always dreamed he would, and he was even healthy, except for that minor business with the haemorrhoids. And yet, Himme wasn't happy – which often made him feel frustrated. His mother, after all, ever since he was a little boy, had always wanted him to be happy.

Something exciting

If Himme could have wished for anything, what would he have wished for?

Quiet? Quiet is serenity, it's a bubble bath, it's grass growing, it's what happens in your refrigerator after you close the door and the little light goes out. In short, quiet is nothingness. And we'll have more than enough of that nothingness eventually, for sure, once we die. For now, Himme felt that what was needed here was something entirely different. Something – never mind what it was called – as long as it tugged at his heart, like the crying of a whale. Something strong, something tough, something dangerous, but still likely to end well. Something that would fill his soul to the brim, causing it to overflow, yet could still be contained. Something exciting, but really exciting, like love, or a mission, or an idea that would take the world forward by light years.

Something like that was just what he needed. At least one, preferably two, urgently, because the guy's dying here in the meantime. And the situation, despite his nonchalant facade, was really and truly serious. 'I heard Suzanne Vega's coming,' his wife said, without looking up from the paper. 'How about it?' 'Why not?' he smiled and wiped the sweat from his face, trying not to let her see how agitated he was. 'Her first record I really liked,' she said. 'The second one not as much, and the third I haven't heard, but everyone says it's lousy. They say she's got a book out too that you can only order online. We could get tickets, and Yael too, I'm sure she'd love to come.'

Yael was a good friend of his wife. Not very pretty, not terribly interesting, but with a very smooth complexion and the nice smell of an easy lay. Once, before he got married, he'd fantasize about that kind of girl, half jerking off, half praying for one to show up. Actually, completely jerking off and completely praying. Not that it did him much good. And today, married and faithful, it really didn't matter anymore.

'Whatever you want, honey,' he said, stressing the *you* almost abjectly.

The tickets were expensive, and the show kind of dull, but moving too. She looked sad when she sang, and it really tugged at Himme's heart. At one point he imagined himself going up on stage and kissing her. An electrifying kiss that would make her his, right then and there. Then she gave an encore. But even though they gave her an ovation, she didn't come out for another number. She went back to America. Maybe suicide, he thought to himself that same night as he tried to maneuver without spilling the drinks he'd gotten for his wife and Yael. Yeah, maybe suicide.

A broken heart

He actually had a relationship once with someone who'd committed suicide. Not emotionally, physically. It happened in the army. He was serving in general staff headquarters at the time, and he'd been brought up on charges for being seen with his boots unpolished. And just when he was walking past the tall staff headquarters building, someone dropped to the ground next to him, splattered. A girl-soldier, they said, with a broken heart, a corporal, Liat Something. Later, he remembered hearing a kind of scream above him as she was falling. But he hadn't looked up. At the time the sound didn't even register.

He reached the hearing all covered in her blood. They let him off. Liat Atlas. That was her name. They even called on him later, to testify at the military police investigation. It couldn't go on this way, that much he knew. Maybe he needed therapy.

Lots of patience

Himme's therapist was hairy.
Himme's therapist took tons of money.
Himme's therapist said it takes lots and lots of patience.
Most of the time he just listened.

When he did say anything, it was usually something dumb, or an annoying question.

It takes lots and lots of patience.

Once he told his therapist, 'Maybe I'll shut up now for a while and you can tell me something about yourself.' And Himme's therapist gave him the tired smile of someone who'd heard that crack more than once, but under the smile it was also obvious that he didn't have much to tell. From the look of it, the only thing working in the therapist's favor was the exhausting allure of mystery. Mystery. Like between a guy and a girl on their first date, that uncertainty, will he try to kiss her, will she agree, and if she does, what will her body look like naked? Mystery was the only card his therapist had up his sleeve, and he wasn't about to give it up so easily.

At that session, neither of them said anything for fifty minutes. Himme spent those fifty minutes imagining his therapist as a beautiful, voluptuous woman, and imagining what would happen if he got up out of his chair and kissed her long, smooth neck. How would she react? A slap? Maybe a half-surprised moan? Except that his therapist wasn't a beautiful, voluptuous woman. 'It takes lots of patience,' he told Himme at the end of that session, as he filled in the invoice, 'lots of patience.' And they both opened their date books and made believe they were really going to meet again.

Science fiction

Once he read an interview with a marriage counselor, who said that in order to rekindle their relationship a couple should clean the bathtub together in the nude, or buy special underwear made of sugar and lick it off one another until it dissolved. Himme and his wife never did things like the complicated ideas he read about in the paper, but still it was obvious that after a very tired half-year they were suddenly on to something. Like in those futuristic movies, where they always have those weapons that track a person's frequency, and the person starts resonating until the special effects come on and everything explodes somehow, he and his wife succeeded in finding some secret frequency in each other too. 'Why don't we go abroad,' his wife purred after one of the times when he came. 'We've never fucked abroad.' 'We fucked in Sinai,' he tried. 'Sinai doesn't count. It's Egypt,' she said, drawing close to him, and kissing him on the eyes. 'Let's go somewhere overseas. Let's go to Greece.'

Here

In the end, they didn't go to Greece. They tried, but it didn't work out – and it was because of her. His job had a special offer on an internet link-

up, and he tried for hours to log on. When he succeeded, he spent most of his time looking for the
names of people he'd known, from work and from
life. Once, on the website of some Dutch anarchist
DJs, he found the name of his upstairs neighbor, or
maybe it was a different Stanislav Hershko. His own
name he couldn't find anywhere, but he discovered
soon enough how to outsmart the system, and slip it
into some sites, and ever since then he'd visited so
many of them, that on his most recent search for
his name he got seventy hits. 'I've got to get out of
here,' he thought, but he also knew that as long as
he wasn't able to figure out what *here* was, he didn't
stand a chance.

Completely alone

One night he had a dream that was
almost prophetic. In the dream, he was in a faraway
country, sitting naked on the sidewalk. In his dream,
he wasn't quite sure what he was doing there. He
looked down at his feet to see if there was any
money on the ground. If there had been any, even a
single coin, he could have thought he was a beggar.
Except that there was nothing. Which made Himme
think that maybe in the dream he was an unsuccess-
ful beggar or maybe even a street performer.
Strange, whenever he dreamed, the thing that

interested him most was his profession. Even in his most abstract dreams, the kind where you lose all your teeth, or where you're drowning, his first thought was always: 'Am I a drowning captain? A naval officer on a missile ship? Maybe a fisherman?' And as he was being swooped up into the whirlpool of his dream, he'd keep struggling, trying to reconstruct, by the items of clothing, what his elusive profession was. Except that in this dream, where he'd been sitting completely naked on the sidewalk, it was obvious that his profession was not the issue. The fact that he was naked was no big deal either. The point about this dream was something altogether different, something that couldn't be referred to by name. The man who was him in the dream was feeling things that couldn't even be put into words, and the real Himme, the one who'd been a visitor in the dream and had only been thinking about professions, was kind of embarrassed that he couldn't be more like him. Strange, Himme thought, to be jealous of your own self in your own dream. And for what? For being naked? For sitting on the sidewalk? For being completely alone?

Other thoughts

In the end she left him. Strange. He'd been having thoughts for such a long time that if

she'd only known about them, she'd have been sob-
bing her heart out or slapping him, or both, and all
that time, while he was looking at her to see if she
could tell, Himme's wife was having thoughts of her
own. From his perspective, they seemed totally inno-
cent: thoughts about cakes and desserts, vacations, a
spa, her mother's health. But in the end, it turned
out that she'd been having other thoughts too,
thoughts that made her leave him. Never mind leave.
Divorce him. If they'd had a kid, they'd probably
have figured out a solution or at least they'd have
kept trying, for the kid's sake. But this way, without a
kid, there wasn't even anyone to make the effort for.

Nissim

In the evening, two days after Himme's
wife left, there was a hesitant knock at the door.
Nonchalantly Himme went to see who it was, trying
not to show any happiness or hope as he opened the
door without checking through the peephole first.
Standing in the doorway were Nissim Roman and
his little daughter, Fortuna, their arms full of dairy
products. 'Our fridge broke down all of a sudden,'
Nissim Roman said shyly. 'It's a crappy fridge. When
the technician comes in the morning, I'll give him
hell. And I thought that maybe in the meantime, if
there's room, we could keep a few things in yours.'

When Himme opened his fridge for them, Nissim tried not to show how sorry he felt for him. 'Lots of room,' he gave Himme an embarrassed smile, and Fortuna arranged the dairy products on one of the empty shelves in neat little stacks. 'We'll take them tomorrow,' Nissim promised, 'bright and early,' and he and Fortuna went home, leaving Himme with himself.

All night long, Himme couldn't fall asleep. And whenever he did, he dreamed how he was stealing into the fridge and drinking the buttermilk that belonged to Nissim Roman and his sad-eyed daughter, and he'd wake up alarmed. There was something scary about how greedy his thoughts were about that buttermilk. Something very scary. The next morning, the little girl came and took everything. Only then did Himme manage to fall asleep. Five minutes later his father phoned, and woke him up.

The Old Guard

If there was one thing that Himme's dad was really good at it was writing eulogies. He had that special knack for pinpointing in the dead the qualities that would make us miss them. When he was young, Himme's dad hadn't had many opportunities to use this extraordinary talent of his. But now that he and his friends had passed seventy, he had his hands full. 'Velvaleh died yesterday,' he told Himme on the phone. 'Your mother hated him, you know, and it's her canasta night besides, so she's not coming. Could you come to the funeral with me by any chance?' Which is how Himme found himself at the cemetery in 32-degree heat, at the open grave of another one of the people his father used to call the Old Guard, listening to an insecure, uncoordinated rabbi recite all sorts of weird mumblings, and waiting patiently for his father to inspire him and the others, the way he always did, with a sense of loss and sorrow. Except that in the case of Velvaleh, Himme was sad to begin with, so that it was a pretty open-and-shut case.

He tried to recall Velvaleh's facial features, which he'd known since childhood, but he didn't do very well. What he did remember, down to the last detail, was his amazing ability to look like just about every other person you've ever known. Every time Himme met him in the street, he'd be sure it was Pinchas, one of his dad's other friends, or Mr Pliskin, who used to own a grocery store on Bialik Street, or all sorts of other people. Himme's dad would always get confused too. Everyone did. Women who wanted to flatter Velvaleh would tell him he reminded them of some movie star, and the truth was that whatever star you picked, he did kind of remind you of him. Beside the open grave Himme's dad said that Velvaleh had grown so used to it, that when he heard someone call out a name in the street, any name, he'd always turn around, because he knew they were really calling him. 'Once, when we were sitting at Café Aviv,' his dad eulogized, his eyes moist, 'Velvaleh asked me if I thought all those people made the same mistake in the other direction too, and called out "Velvaleh! Velvaleh!" in the street when they saw someone else.'

A house without roaches

Nissim Roman and his little daughter were standing there, in the back yard of his building, staring, transfixed, at a man in a T-shirt that read 'The Eichmann of Roaches'. It had a picture underneath of a giant roach floundering on its back. The exterminator was trying to lift the lid of the sewer, and went on telling the Romans how the Chief Entomologist of the Ministry of Health had once told him that there was no such thing as a house without roaches. There are always some roaches, but because they only show up in the dark, you don't notice them next to you. And by the time you do, even if it's only one or two, it really means there are lots of them. And sure enough, right under the lid of the sewer, there were like a million roaches scurrying every which way. 'Yikes!' little

Fortuna shrieked, and ran away, and Nissim Roman scrambled after her in his flip-flops. The only ones left in the yard now were the exterminator, a frightened swarm of roaches in their final death throes, and Himme sweating like crazy in the drab suit his dad had insisted on lending him. 'From one funeral to the next, eh?' the exterminator stopped spraying the sewer for a moment and pointed at Himme's head. That's when Himme realized he was still wearing the cardboard yarmulke they gave him at the cemetery.

Ten times more

Once or twice a day, Himme would snoop on his ex-wife, peeking into her new apartment from one of the trees facing it. Most of the time, she wasn't doing anything special. Just the kind of stuff he knew about from when they were married: TV, lots of books, taking in a movie with Yael. After her shower, she'd stare at her figure in the mirror, pinching herself all over, and making cute faces. The truth was that it was very easy to like her during this ceremony, and Himme wondered if this was something new or whether she'd always done it but he just hadn't noticed, because he'd only started snooping on her after they broke up. Maybe, he thought, there are lots of things about her that

I don't know, and if I'd known about those things when we were still married, I'd have loved her ten times more. And me too. Maybe there are a million cute things like that about me, and if she'd known about them, she'd never have wanted to leave me. Who knows – maybe lots of nice things had gone on between them, showing up in the dark, like the roaches, and the fact that they'd gone unnoticed still didn't mean that they weren't there.

V.A.T.

'Think about it,' Himme's dad said once, 'I've never been to India, and you've always wanted to go there. Your mother said she'd be glad to have a break from me for a few weeks too. Whaddya say?' And when he saw Himme hesitating, he continued: 'Look, me, my life is over. All I have left now is the V.A.T. Without lots of commitments, without lots of worries. With a couple of short espressos, some quality time with my adorable son, and maybe, if it fits in, even a little elephant trek. And you too, Son, what have you got to do around here anyway? How much longer can you keep peeping at your ex-wife in the shower? Either they'll arrest you in the end, or you'll fall out of a tree. Wouldn't it be better to spend some time with your dad, to visit one of the Seven Wonders of the World with your dad?'

India

The revolving restaurant on the rooftop of their Delhi hotel looped only one song, Frank Sinatra's 'My Way'. Over and over again, at every meal, three meals a day. For Himme, the cumulative effect of the cumulative listening to the cumulative song was cumulatively distressing. Himme's dad took it in his stride, and even kept whistling along with Sinatra over and over, but Himme refused to resign himself to this fate, and on their third day he demanded an explanation. 'Why the same song?' he took it up with the manager. The smiling Indian shook his head slowly the way Indians do: 'This is like asking why same restaurant go round and round. Restaurant go round and round because this is best restaurant in Delhi. Same with song. "My Way" – best song, and we play only best song in best restaurant in Delhi.'

'Yes, but there are other songs. Also good songs,' Himme attempted.

'"My Way" best song,' the manager repeated his mantra with smiling resolve. 'No second best for my guests.'

Ramat Gan

Outside the revolving restaurant, the world seemed even stranger, and Himme found himself sticking to the hotel room, while his father made valiant sorties into the outside world and came back armed with new experiences and leprous friends, who were glad to join him in the elevator to the fourteenth floor and to meet his very talented, albeit somewhat depressive son.

When he felt he'd exhausted Delhi, Himme's dad dragged his plaintive son northwards, to breath-takingly beautiful villages, where even Himme began to enjoy himself. The beauty, and the generosity and openness of the Indians along with Himme's dad's Old Guard stories all came together in his mind, in an overwhelming but incredibly moving jumble. And so, riding an elephant at sun-set, he heard the sad life story of the meticulously well mannered boxer who'd come to Ramat Gan all the way from Freiburg, Germany and established Atom-Bar from scratch, and how, with a single terrible left hook and half a heart he'd knocked down both Sinkevitch brothers, even though deep down inside him he believed that knocking down clients would be bad luck, and indeed three years later the bar was burned to the ground by a tattooed Maori gentile after a local hooker had insulted him.

Turned out the Indians loved Himme's dad's stories too. They listened very closely, and usually laughed in the right places, which sometimes helped Himme forget that they hadn't understood a word.

A closer study revealed that rather than listening, they were actually concentrating on his dad's glorious bare potbelly, and the way it shimmied whenever he described something particularly funny or moving. On the underside of his dad's belly there was a scar from when he'd had his appendix out, and one of the Indians told Himme in broken English that every time the scar turned red, they knew the story had taken a very dangerous turn. Himme's dad took this whole audience in stride, and kept on reminiscing out loud, while swallowing the saliva that filled his mouth as he carried on about Shiyya Barbalat, the legendary wandering junkman from Hamavdil Street, who'd sneaked around town with his horse and carriage one night, and beheaded all the 'No Horses Allowed' signs, then scattered their ravaged carcasses in the back yard of the Municipal Department of Motor Vehicles. Interesting what the Indians would think if they could actually understand. They would probably imagine this Ramat Gan as an exotic place. Fact is that even to Himme, who'd grown up on Hashalom Road, just three kilometers from where all those stories took place, his dad's Ramat Gan sounded like something far away – not just in space and in time, but also in a million other dimensions that he couldn't even name.

Like himself

Himme's dad's death came out of no-where. Suddenly his dad was feeling 'under the weather', suddenly a dizziness, suddenly a fever, suddenly they needed a doctor but there wasn't a doctor to be found. Drink a lot, stay in the room and rest. Himme's dad kept smiling the whole time. The fever, he'd tell Himme, was actually pleasant. 'It's like after a bottle of rye,' he'd laugh, 'only without the upset stomach.' When Himme was alone with him, it seemed like nothing, but judging by the concern of the Indian who was renting them the room, it was obviously serious. Himme's dad was calm, and he wasn't just pretending, but that didn't really say anything about the situation. It wasn't about dying, after all, just about getting a rebate on your V.A.T. His life was over a long time ago anyway, and everything that happened after that was an add-on, a kind of quality adventure with his adorable son on the wide tax bracket of time.

After his dad died, Himme buried him in the back yard of the house where they were staying. The Indian landlord tried to persuade him it would be better to have the body cremated, but when he saw that Himme was adamant, he got some spades and dug along with him. By the time they'd finished covering the grave, it was evening, and Himme was busy taking care of a blister that had developed on the thumb of his digging hand, and wondering what to inscribe on the tombstone. Strange how his dad had been so good at eulogies, and he couldn't even come up with a single sentence. The only thing that occurred to him in connection with his dad was that he was utterly like himself. Lots of thoughts got all jumbled in his head, some of them telling him that it had been a mistake to bury his father there, and that he should have taken the body back home, and that he ought to call right away, call his mother, whom he was missing a lot, and maybe his ex-wife too, who had loved Himme's dad very much, and that maybe this sad situation would cause her to come back to him, at least for a short while, out of pity. Other thoughts had to do with Barbalat, with Velvaleh, with Atom-Bar, with that whole world that Himme had never known and that Himme's dad had just been united with. And there were also thoughts about passports and rupees, and about what's-going-to-happen-now, and another tiny glimpse – about how life had protected him until now, like a Fabergé egg in a padded box, and about how in his entire thirty-two years it had hardly confronted him with anyone who'd died (two people): his dad, and the girl-soldier with the broken heart who'd fallen to the ground beside him at staff head-quarters. He sat and waited for all those thoughts to pass, but when he realized that they were just going on and on, he got up, stuck a piece of wood in the mound, took a black felt-tip pen and wrote 'The Old Guard' in bold print.

Fortuna

Even after his dad died, Himme kept on roaming around India, with no particular goal in mind. Some of the time he felt bored or shitty, for no reason. Lots of times he felt happiness, and for no particularly good reason either. In one small town, not far from Oranjabad, he met an Indian girl who looked exactly like his neighbor's daughter, Fortuna. She was playing hopscotch with another little girl, slightly older, and just like Fortuna Roman, the Indian Fortuna stayed serious all through the game, and even when she won, her eyes stayed sad. After the game he followed her home, and saw that the Indian Fortuna also lived in a parterre apartment, on the left. Because he'd kept his distance as he followed her, he couldn't see who opened the door for her when she rang the bell. The voice of whoever opened it spoke Hindi, but it sounded surprisingly like Nissim Roman. Which meant that the apartment opposite theirs might just belong to the Indian Himme. And Himme was terribly eager to knock on his door, but he didn't have the nerve.

He sat on the stairs and tried to imagine what life must be like for the Indian Himme behind that door. And how much like him he really was. Whether he was divorced, whether his father was alive, whether his father had stories about Oranjabad of earlier days too, and whether his wife's Indian girlfriend also had the smell of an easy lay. Three hours later, the door opened and out came a grim young Indian with a handlebar mustache. He looked at Himme and Himme looked at him without lowering their gaze. After a few seconds, Himme was feeling so uneasy that he got up and left. Deep in his heart, he hoped that the sad Indian was nothing at all like him.

No attachment

The whole time Himme was wandering aimlessly, he didn't phone his mother back home even once, and it made him feel guilty and mean. He didn't phone his ex-wife either, or anyone else actually. All in all, he didn't talk to too many people in India altogether, and he spent most of his time on his own. Until he reached the guesthouse in Puna, where a group of three Israeli *sannyasis* started talking to him in Hebrew about Existence, against his will. The most talkative of the lot was called Bashir. Sometimes the other *sannyasis* called him

Moshe, but he'd correct them. Bashir told Himme
that you could tell at a glance he was far from his
center, and that this was very sad, because Bashir
had also been far from his center once, and he'd
studied at the College of Business Administration,
and only now, in retrospect, when he'd found half
the light, did he understand how terribly he'd been
suffering. Himme tried to pretend in English that he
didn't understand what Bashir was saying and that
he was really a tourist from Italy, but his accent was a
giveaway. 'Man,' Bashir placed his hand on Himme's
shoulder, 'you've got to be more trusting. To get in
touch with yourself. Don't you realize what's happening to you? you're in a flip.' And Himme, who
really was not in touch with what was happening to
him, or with what 'in a flip' meant, moved even fur-
ther away from his center and tried to sock Bashir in
the jaw, but he missed and slipped, and banged his
head against the edge of the table, just at the very
moment when the three *sannyasis* spotted two
German chicks and rushed over to offer them a
tantral relationship with no attachment, that would
help them connect to their true selves.

Flip

The truth is that Moshe, or Bashir, or
whatever his name was, had a point, and Himme

really had flipped. He was angry, and he was bored, and he was homesick, and he was so much of all of those that he thought he was going to explode. He felt himself a victim, he felt himself to blame, he felt himself upstanding, he felt he had no name, and even more than he was feeling, he was thinking.

A typical thought by way of example: at night, when we say we're going to sleep, and we get into bed and shut our eyes, we're not really asleep. We're just pretending. We shut our eyes and breathe rhythmically, pretending to be asleep, until the deceit slowly becomes real. And maybe that's how it is with death. Himme's dad didn't die right away either. And the whole time when his eyes were shut and he wasn't moving, you could still feel his pulse. Maybe Himme's dad was going to die just like someone would be going to sleep – he was just pretending, until it became real. And if so, then it was very possible that if Himme had interrupted him in the process, jumped on his bed like a little kid, opened one of his eyes to make sure, shouted 'Dad!' and tickled him, the whole deceit would simply have failed.

Grazie

Himme returned to his room, his forehead bleeding. He didn't have a first-aid kit, and he didn't really feel like looking for the guesthouse owner and asking him for one either. Near the door to his room, he bumped into a tourist who seemed kind of familiar. She told him in broken English that she was French, and that she'd be glad to lend him a bandage. He told her he was Italian, and even added 'Grazie' at the end. But both of them knew for sure that they were Israelis who were tired of meeting other Israelis in the East. So she helped him with the bandage, in English, and he smiled at her, and tried to remember where he knew her from. In the end, without either of them really planning it, they fucked. And afterwards, when they'd already told each other their real names, he knew. 'Sivan Atlas?' he smiled a crooked smile. 'I think I met your sister once, may she rest in peace, but just for a second.'

At night Sivan cried, and at least from the outside it seemed to be helping her feel better, and so did Himme. He let go of his tears like a hot-air balloon jettisons another extra-heavy bag of sand, and as they lay there in each other's arms, he could imagine how if only he'd let go of her, he'd start floating up towards the ceiling. The next morning, Sivan continued to Dharamsala according to plan, and Himme, who didn't have one, remained.

One serious mind-fuck

He lit himself a cigarette. Until recently he'd still been trying to quit, but by now he'd seen enough of the light to understand it didn't really matter. 'Would you happen to have another one, for me too?' asked his Baba, a compulsive miser and a bit of a nuisance. 'No,' he lied. 'It's my last one.' A particularly good-looking Dutch trekker stopped beside them, looking for a hostel. And the Baba gave her some vague reply about how the whole world is really one big hostel, and managed, as if just in passing, to get an unfiltered Lucky Strike and a pack of sugarless gum out of her. He also tried to work up a conversation, but when he saw she wasn't into it, he reverted to spirituality. 'Beautiful, eh?' the Baba smiled at him. 'Sure,' Himme nodded. 'But what difference does it make, Baba, I don't really exist anyway, do I?' 'You'd make it with her, eh?' the Baba sniggered, and took a drag on his Lucky Strike. 'How can I make it with her if I don't really exist?' he stabbed back, 'if she doesn't really exist? Believe me, this whole existence thing is just one serious mind-fuck. You're a Baba. You of all people should know what I mean.' 'I'd screw her brains out,' the Baba persisted, not listening. Strange, that of all the Babas that Shiva had scattered around the world, Himme had to go and choose the only one who was also a cab driver. Countless roads lead to enlightenment. Buddha, for example, reached Nirvana through despair, Chang-Chu through in-action. It would be interesting to find out what his Baba's road was. Reality grew sharper around him, deionizing itself of every bit of dirt or haziness, as he began sinking into a state of no-mind. 'I need some more money, for dhal,' the Baba nudged him gently till he responded, and then returned to eat it next to him, taking care not to get his clothes dirty. 'Where do you think that Dutch chick went?' he asked with his mouth full. 'She didn't really exist,' Himme insisted, 'she was just a thought.' And the Baba, who'd become thirsty again, borrowed some money from him for a Coke. 'Once,' he said, 'I got laid by some tourist. Nothing great, kind of fat. But she kept laughing the whole time. I love it when girls laugh.' Himme felt how everything around him was beginning to fade away, like an old thought, like a memory that's almost been forgot-ten. 'I'll be back in a minute,' the Baba said, 'I just want to look into something.' And even though he knew that time was just an illusion, Himme nodded. 'If you give me a little cash, I'll buy us some cigarettes,' the Baba said and started playing around with the sole of his shoe. 'Look at my shoes, completely torn. So how about that Dutch babe, didn't she seem interested?' While the Baba was off buying cigarettes, Buddha arrived to visit him, smiling and chubby as always, with the tip of a familiar scar showing on the underside of his potbelly, and Buddha even brought him a present – a wicker basket full of puffballs. He blew on one of the puffballs, and the whole world disappeared.

SECOND CHANCE

On the face of it, it seemed like just another service – innovative, revolutionary, monstrous, call it whatever you want – but when you came right down to it, *Second Chance* was the greatest economic success story of the twenty-first century. Unlike most great ideas, which tend to be quite simple, the idea behind *Second Chance* was a bit more complicated: *Second Chance* gave you the opportunity to go to one particular critical moment in your life, and instead of having to choose either one road or the other, you could continue along both. Can't decide whether to have the abortion and drop your boyfriend, or to marry him and start a family? Not sure whether you should start from scratch overseas, or stay put in your dad's business? Now you can have it both ways! How does it work? Well, it's like this: you've reached the most important crossroad in your life and you can't make up your mind? Just head for the *Second Chance* outlet nearest your home and give them a full rundown on your dilemma. Then choose one of the options, whichever you want, and keep on living your life. Don't worry, the other option, the one you didn't choose, doesn't disappear. They have it running on one of their *If-Only-I'd* computers (Reg. Tr.), carefully keeping track of all the variables. Once you've gone through your life in full, your body is taken to one of the *Road-Not-Taken* halls (also Reg. Tr.), where the entire data set is fed into your brain in real time, and kept alive through a unique bio-electronic process developed expressly for this purpose. So actually, your own brain can give you the experience of the other life you could have had, down to the last detail.

Miri or Shiri? Teary or cheery?
Placid old age or perhaps hara kiri?
A child or a pup? IVF or adopt?
Move to Miami or pick up where you stopped?
At *Second Chance*, whatever you do,
You can have your cake and eat it too.

It's perfect. Seriously. Nothing cynical about it. It's a fabulous concept. I mean, there aren't many inventions that actually succeed in meeting some human need. Ninety-nine per cent of them are just some ugly combo of pushy marketing and spineless consumers. And *Second Chance* is clearly in that single significant, useful percentile. Except what does that have to do with Max?

Our Max lived his life straight as an arrow, fast as lightning, no ifs, no buts, at least until now. Max's dad – well, that's a different story altogether. Max's dad not only opted for *Second Chance*, he never stopped talking about it either: 'If it weren't for that rotten *Second Chance*, I'd never – and I do mean never – have married that revolting mother of yours,' he'd tell Max at least once a day. 'I swear, sometimes I feel like putting a bullet through my head, just so I can finally make it to *Road-Not-Taken*.' (By the way, a bullet through the head specifically is a very poor choice. *Second Chance* assumes absolutely no responsibility for the quality of service in case of major damage to cerebral tissue.) Max knew that his father didn't really mean it, and he hoped that his mother realized this too, but even if she did, it didn't make his dad's behavior any less upsetting. 'If he'd taken the *Second Chance* in connection with my being born instead,' Max tried to console her, 'he'd have been just as obsessive: "I feel like putting a

217

bullet through my head just so I can re-live my life without that egotistical kid. If I went and died tomorrow I bet he wouldn't even bother coming to the funeral." You know how Dad is, it has nothing to do with you.'

The truth is that his mother really did opt for *Second Chance* in connection with having him, but she was tactful enough never to let on about it. In her case, the *Road-Not-Taken* would have led her to a quick divorce, a successful business venture and a happy second marriage. No harm done, she'd get a chance to live that life too.

Max had always preferred women who were curvy, tan, with big tits and thick lips. And Shana, who was very very pretty, by the way, was the complete opposite. She was skinny, flat as a board, and her lips were about as thick as a credit card. But love, as the saying goes, is blind, and Max fell in love. Before the wedding they didn't opt for *Second Chance*, or before the twins either. Max was against it in principle. He said people ought to assume responsibility for their own decisions. And as for Shana, she'd already wasted hers long before that on a previous boyfriend, whose proposal she'd turned down in her regular life. The thought that after her death she'd experience marriage with someone else was pretty frustrating as far as Max was concerned, but it was also motivational. And the need to feel that he was the right choice often drove him to be a better husband.

Years later, about six months after Shana had used up her first chance and had left Max on his own, his grandchildren asked him what his *Second Chance* had been, and he said he hadn't had one. They didn't believe him. 'Grandpa's a liar,' they shouted. 'Grandpa's embarrassed.' People had almost stopped using *Second Chance* by then, and had moved on to *Meeny Miny Mo*, which gave you an intriguing third option to explore, at no extra charge.

'Cause two birds in the bush
Can't beat three – all for you.
Take *Meeny Miny* and *Mo*
And your wishes come true.